Praise for the Base Branch Series

"Megan Mitcham's books are well-paced, well-plotted suspense novels edged with stunning sensual intensity. Her lovers are cold and deadly--except when they are skin-to-skin. I can't wait for the next book in the series!"

- **DELILAH DEVLIN**
New York Times and USA Today bestselling author

"A true gift from an exceptional storyteller.."

- **CRISTIN HARBER**
New York Times and USA Today bestselling author

"This is a fresh and exciting story with lots of great characters."

- **5 Star Amazon Review**, Enemy Mine

"Megan now joins my elite team of must read authors. I fell in love with her work in *Enemy Mine*, and it just gets better the more I read."

- **TNT Reviews**

BOOKS BY MEGAN MITCHAM

BASE BRANCH NOVELS
ENEMY MINE
JUSTICE MINE
STRANGER MINE
WARRIOR MINE
DANGER MINE
PRISONER MINE
VERSIONS
VIRTUES
VARIATIONS
NEVER MINE
FURIOUSLY MINE
RELENTLESSLY MINE
CAPTOR MINE
SURVIVOR MINE

BUREAU NOVELS
FOR ALL TO SEE
PAINTED WALLS

ANTHOLOGIES
ANTICIPATION
CONQUESTS
ROGUES
SEX OBJECTS
COWBOY HEAT
HIGH OCTANE HEROES
WILD AT HEART VOLUME II
benefiting Turpentine Creek Wildlife Refuge

Never Mine

Base Branch Novella #10

Megan Mitcham

Published by MM Publishing LLC

Edited by Jenny Sims

Proofread by Tina Rucci & Lynn Mullan

Cover Design by Deranged Doctor Designs

Virtues
All Rights Are Reserved. Copyright 2017 by Megan Mitcham

Never Mine

Publication: January 2017

Digital ISBN: 978-1-941899-28-1

Print ISBN: 978-1-941899-29-8

To Cristin Harber,

Thank you beyond words for creating characters and a world I love almost as much as my own and inviting me to play in it with them. This book was the easiest I've ever written because it was the ultimate version of playing with your friend's toys.

Your Forever Fan,

Megan

Dear Readers,

Welcome to the Titan World books with stories ranging from military romance to paranormal to contemporary romance. There's something for everyone—action-packed romance, swoon-worthy moments, and happily ever after!

When I started the Titan series, I wanted to combine my love of steamy romance and action-packed suspense. I wrote strong men and women who I hoped readers would fall in love with. I can't think of anything more exciting than opening my world up to very talented authors to extend that experience so that you, the reader, can have a deeper connection to more than one book series at a time.

You will meet new characters and see them interact with familiar ones; you will also see the interpretation of the Titan universe through another author's eyes. I hope that you take the time to experience each book in the Titan World series!

You are in for a treat with Megan Mitcham's *Never Mine*, where her Base Branch Special Forces hero meets the Titan Group in a romantic suspense tale that is as hot as the desert it's set in. When Megan and I first sat down over dinner to talk about the possibility of our worlds colliding, the opportunity seemed incredible. Now that I've read this story, I can promise you, *Never Mine* is a true gift from an exceptional storyteller.

Thank you to Megan and all the authors who took time out of their busy writing schedules to participate in this project. I think the result is something truly special for our readers.

Titan Hugs and Happy Reading,
Cristin Harber

Chapter One

Solid weight pinned Jillian to the bed. His arms lay heavily over her arms. His long legs tangled with hers. Coarse hairs tickled her skin, taunting her with the need to move, to writhe. His torso fluctuated with frantic breaths. Her lungs reveled in the opportunity to breathe him in. The scent of sweat and the musk of sex ratcheted her desire for this man. Unyielding slabs of muscle pressed her ample breasts flat, except for her nipples. They pierced his rough, tattooed skin with lustful defiance.

"You come when I order you to come, and not a moment sooner, you devil." He growled her nickname against her earlobe, tempting her rebellion.

What would he do if she disobeyed? What would he withhold? The latter thought kept her need for control at bay.

"Yes, Callum."

Her lips grazed the perpetual stubble on his neck. If only she had the reach to drag them over his jaw to his lips. The full things looked like the perfect pillows for her own wide mouth.

"That's better."

The point of his jaw scraped her neck to her clavicle. Her heart clapped wildly against her sternum in celebration. If his lips or teeth grazed a nipple, she might disintegrate in the effort it would take not to succumb to an orgasm. His weight lifted, and she arched in a desperate search for his touch.

His palm and fingers spread wide against her sternum and pushed her back to the silky cotton. He hovered over her. St. Michael stared at her from his bicep. The Archangel's spear pierced the fallen devil on his forearm and ushered three souls into the clouds and shafts of light on his large shoulder.

"Eyes on me, not Michael."

Callum's fingertips bit into her thigh and shoved it wide. His knee spread her other leg, leaving her exposed. Sultry night air kissed her folds with flaming lips.

"He won't make you come."

Jillian banked a whimper. The need to grind against him charged again without permission. Her hips ground the open air, begging him to fill her. Muscles inside her wet pussy contracted with unchecked greed.

"You are the devil, Jillian. You tempt me to move faster than you need, but one day, you'll learn. I know exactly what you need."

A carved shin planted on both of her thighs. Her long grinding turned to pitiful twitches. Tears cooled her cheeks.

"Please, Callum. I need you."

"I know what you need, Devil." His eyes darkened from coffee brown to midnight black. "You need my Trident."

She needed anything he would give. She needed it to take her next breath. She needed it to face another day. She needed him.

His right shoulder rolled forward. Poseidon, god of the sea, rose from the water and glowered at her. Every etched muscle leaned into the handle, into the strike of the three points of his Trident. Callum's hand slid between her folds and buried two fingers deep inside her flesh. The sharpest spear of the skewer pointed at the tip of her clit.

"Yes. Oh, Callum. Don't stop."

Jillian arched into him as much as his imprisoning hold would allow. He loomed over her, the scared gargoyle to his tattooed arms. She'd never witnessed anything more beautiful than the danger in his eyes, the lust on his fingertips, and the acreage of minutely defined muscles that punctuated his every inch.

He found the sensitive spot inside her pussy and milked it with hard, steady strokes. The tingling started in her toes. She shook her head in a near delirious back and forth. More than almost anything, she wanted the orgasm that terrorized her with the promise of ecstasy. Only one thing came before.

Pleasing Callum came before she did, literally.

Sweat beaded on her forehead and rolled between her breasts.

"That's right, Devil. Not yet. I know what you need. When you're ready, I'll give it to you."

"I'm ready. Oh. I'm so ready."

"Let me see." He slid his fingers from her body, slicked them over her clit, and lifted them to his mouth. The red of his sinful tongue lolled out and then curled up the pads of his fingers. A deep rumble emanated from his chest and filled her ears. "Almost, but not quite."

Callum fisted his cock, pumped the hard flesh twice, and then danced the broad head in circles around her wet folds. The circles grew smaller at a maddening pace. Her breaths condensed on her chest, adding to the obscene heat. Finally, his wide head reached the bull's-eye. He paid close attention to her clit, lashing the swollen nub again and again. She pressed against his hand on her chest and got nowhere. A sinister smile lifted his mouth.

"Now, you taste and tell me if you're ready." He grabbed the back of her neck and one leg and dragged her ninety degrees. The pink head of his cock slicked with her desire bobbed inches from her face.

Her cheeks flamed, and her mouth watered. Finally free to do as she pleased, Jillian levered off the bed onto an elbow. She opened her lips wide.

"Ah." Callum shifted his hips away from her mouth.

Her heart sank. She swallowed, found his gaze, and begged without words.

"Just a taste. Don't be greedy."

"Yes, Callum." Her gaze fell to his cock.

He pushed forward again. A drop of pre-cum wept from his slit. The salt of his arousal and the tang of her own rich excitement coated her tongue as he slid inside. Her inner muscles clenched. She moaned long and hard.

"Good, Little Devil."

He nodded his approval and twisted her around until her ass bloomed in front of his dick. The heavy weight of his flesh pressed against her opening.

"Please, Callum."

Tears streamed down her cheek. Why was she crying? The moisture chilled her to the bone, yet she boiled from the inside out.

Callum leaned back.

"No. Don't leave."

He climbed from the bed.

"No." Jillian's voice echoed in the small confines of her dark, empty bedroom.

The irritating trill of electronic birds chirped from her phone on the nightstand. Her limbs weighed a thousand pounds, eyelids too. Sleep clouded her vision. They closed out the morning and tempted her back to the scene of the crime. She reached blindly to hit the snooze on the alarm.

Cotton sheets stroked her erect nipples. That simple contact awakened her naked form to full, aching awareness. Moisture slicked her thighs. Her swollen folds pulsed.

Jillian slapped away the tears chilling her cheek. If it had been anyone else in her dream, she'd finish herself off and call it a win. But even now, temptation loomed. She pulled the covers over her shoulders to keep out the cold as her fingers glided over her abdomen. A thrill rushed ahead of her touch and coursed straight between her legs.

She danced her other hand over her breasts but avoided the hotspots of her nipples. It wouldn't take much. In fact, she was pretty damn sure she'd already come. He was gone, but his presence, his touch, still loomed large over her sweat soaked body.

Never before had she finished herself off with him. Never should she, but the pull dragged at her. A year of running from it had left her starved.

Again, her alarm chirped.

"It's the weekend," Jillian snarled at her phone and leaned over to silence the damn thing. She'd just wrapped up training at the US Naval Academy and wasn't due to give her workshop at Quantico until next Monday. The reminder had flashed on her screen a second before she slapped the alarm.

Every warm and sexy thought froze solid, fell to the floor, and shattered into a million pieces. She'd almost willingly gone back to the crime scene.

A bloody outline of a body should be on her floor because the damned dreams killed something inside her every time. As long as she didn't speak of them, there was no proof they existed. Unless her flailing heart inside her chest counted.

Today was Amery's six-month anniversary.

Jillian's stomach cramped. She stumbled out of bed and ran to the bathroom. The toilet seat hit the back of the commode with a whack. Her palms clung to the cold bowl, while her long brown hair curtained her misery. Breaths sucked in through her nose flew out her mouth, waiting for the inevitable dry heaves. She reveled in the sickness. It showed she still thought her mind a treacherous bastard.

When the vomit refused to show, her tears took its place. One by one, they created ripples in the water. This wasn't the time for tears. If she didn't get ready now, she'd be late. She stood, turned on the shower, and stared at her reflection in the mirror.

Bloodshot brown eyes stared back at long hair matted to her head and blotchy tearstained cheeks. She went to war with less emotion than this. And today would be a battle.

It was time to prepare for war—a purely internal one, but a ferocious fight all the same.

Chapter Two

"Daddy!" The shrill whistle of Aria's angry voice put an RPG to shame. "No. You can't have it. It's mine. Daddy!"

Callum straightened the already precisely positioned SEAL Trident above his bars and heart. He took one last look in his mirror at the dress blues weighing heavily on his shoulders and then headed toward the cacophony.

My Little Pony's intro blasted from the flat screen hanging on Ashlyn's pink wall in her pink room with her pink bed and her sparkly pink curtains. Every time he set eyes on the Pepto-Bismol décor, a smile twisted one side of his mouth. He stepped over a tablet screaming about Play-Doh eggs and prize packs. Past Aria's more sedate yet also pink room, he found the girls.

They rolled across the living room carpet in their Sunday best. Ashlyn held her little fist outstretched, placed her thumb at the cleft of Aria's nose, and shoved. Aria blocked the tiny but determined hand and lunged for the trinket clutched in Ashlyn's tiny hand.

He couldn't help the pride welling inside his chest. Girls or not, these two would be lethal by age twelve. Boys, beware.

"No!" Ashlyn flailed her entire body, making big waves for a three-year-old.

"It's mine." Aria pried each tiny finger, one at a time, and ripped a bracelet from her sister's grip. "You could have broken it."

Ash pulled one full breath, her already pink cheeks reddened, and the wailing began. Fat tears cascaded over a scrunched face. Her stuttered inhale bruised his already tender heart.

"What's going on?" He held himself at attention before passing judgment or giving comfort. It was the toughest part of being a parent —a single parent—of two feisty girls.

Ashlyn smoothed her dress and hair and then mirrored his stance. "Aria stole the bracelet that Momma gave me from my room, and she refused to give it back."

"Thank you for your concise answer." He nodded.

"What does concise mean?" One thin blond brow arched.

"Succinct." When that didn't relax the brow, he added, "To the point."

"Oh." Ashlyn's straight hair swayed around her shoulders.

Aria continued to sob on the floor.

Callum walked to her side and waited. And waited. Finally, she shivered with one last hurrah, wiped her eyes, and looked up at him.

"Is it true?" She sucked in a breath and opened her mouth wide. He held up one hand. "Remember, before you answer, your integrity is everything." Her nose wrinkled. "Your word," he explained.

"Oh." She sighed and wiped at her full rosy cheeks. "I stoled it."

"Stole it," he corrected.

"Yeah." The word turned into a cry.

He scooped his baby girl up into his arms and rocked her from foot to foot until the quaking slowed. "Thank you for telling me the truth."

Aria nodded against his coat, rubbing tears and snot onto the shoulder. He'd had worse on the thing. Well, on his other ones, not the dress blues, but it didn't matter.

"Why'd you take the bracelet, Aria?" he whispered into her ear.

"I wanted to habit."

"Have it?" he clarified.

"Yeah." Aria sniffled, dragged her fist across her nose, and wiped it on his collar.

"Because?"

"It was pretty on Momma."

Losing Amery had been hard but doable. He was a SEAL, after all. Adapting and moving forward had been embedded into his brain and sewn into his every repetition for so long, he did it without thinking. Days like these—when he realized how much his daughters hurt for their mom—were the hardest.

"I have an idea." Callum chucked the chubby point of her chin and winked.

"What is it?" She eyed him skeptically.

"How about we go find you a bracelet from Momma's jewelry drawer."

"Oooh." Aria covered her mouth. "We're not supposed to go into Momma's drawers. You'll get in trouble."

"If I say it's okay, then it's okay. This once." He planted a kiss on his baby's head and marched them toward the bedroom.

The life she gave the room had dwindled over the months. Most days, Callum felt little when he entered.

Today, he was aware of everything. Amery's soft taste covered the walls in paintings of poppy covered fields, in the thick white curtains and comforter, and in the collage of family photos that covered every inch of her dresser.

"Look!" Aria's pudgy little finger pointed. "Momma, Jilly Billy, Ashlyn, and me at the beach. I want to go to the beach again, Daddy. The waves flewed me a long way. Can you come this time? You and Jilly Billy. I know Momma can't come, but we can go. Can we?"

Callum stared at the last photo taken of his beautiful wife before...

She and Jillian stood in front of the surf with their toes buried in the sand, looking hot as hell in teeny-weeny bikinis. The women contrasted in almost every way. Amery towered a foot over Jilly, while Jilly's curves made Amery look like a rail—a sexy rail, but a rail all the same. Their coloring and even their personalities clashed, but they had a tighter relationship than the best sniper spotter teams he'd met.

Ashlyn sat atop Jilly's muscled shoulders. In his oldest daughter's eyes and personal disposition, he saw himself; brown and stalwart. She had Amery's hair, as did Aria, who propped atop her mother's shoulders like her own personal mini-me. Every girl donned a laughing smile that both warmed his heart and chilled it.

They'd been so happy, and he'd missed out on the contagious joy for the spraying bullets and battle cries of his enemies.

"Can we, Daddy?" Ashlyn tugged on the hem of his coat. Her eyes lit with hope. A fraction of the smile she boasted in the picture curved her precious mouth and restored his hope that they would see that level of joy again.

He wanted to promise them the trip more than the world, but Jillian had kept her distance lately. Whether they were the sad reminders of all she'd lost or work really was that busy, the fact remained.

"I'd like that, but we'll have to see, girls."

Their disappointment deflated the room. Before it completely collapsed around them, he pulled open the coveted jewelry drawer. Curiosity instantaneously rebounded their moods.

"Wow." Ashlyn sighed.

"I want that one and that one and that one and..." Aria went down the rows claiming each of them.

"Not fair. If she can have more than one, I want more too." Ashlyn reached into the drawer.

"Wait." He commanded a team of the most elite soldiers in the world but lost control of his girls quickly and often. "Aria, you may pick two things. Ashlyn, you may pick one thing, since you already have the bracelet your mom gave you. Understood?"

"Yes, sir." Ashlyn snagged a costume necklace with chains that cascaded to a point.

"Yes, sir." Aria dove headfirst into the drawer. He had caught her ham hocks before she smashed her face on a thickly wrapped set of pink beads his wife had worn exactly one time. She'd chosen the flashy things to go with a white cocktail dress for a springtime rooftop party in downtown D.C. before Aria had been a concrete thought. Aria grabbed the matching bracelet.

"Everyone happy now?" He righted Aria and eyed them both. The girls nodded. "Great. Let's go see Jilly and Momma."

"Can we go visit Boo again?" Aria whined.

"Boomer," Ashlyn corrected.

"We're due for another visit, soon." Callum needed to see Jillian for more than a sense of familial health. He needed to grow his surprise idea on her.

Aria wiggled out of his arms. A clacking herd of tiny high heels thundered out of the room and down the hallway. He followed them, turning off the myriad of electronics and lights left in their wake, and fastened them both into the back of his shiny black pickup. They drove the quiet Washington streets. The girls only managed to ask a hundred questions each before they pulled down the gently winding path and parked.

Jillian stood next to her own shiny black pickup. The damn truck brought a smile to his face. They'd argued their respective brand loyalty and merits until Amery had threatened to beat both vehicles with baseball bats if they didn't stow it. Jilly promptly reminded Amery that she didn't own a baseball bat, to which Amery told her bandage scissors and medical tape would work just fine.

In the backseat, the girls squealed. Ashlyn's seatbelt hit the wall. She wiggled out of her booster and lunged at Aria, making fast work of her sister's five-point harness. Before he turned off the truck, both girls had bailed. He could see them one day not too long from now trying a tuck and roll from a moving vehicle just for the hell of it.

"Jilly!" The girls' screams filtered through the glass and metal, accentuating just how long it had been since they'd seen the woman who'd been a second mother to them. Hell, when Amery had deployed after having Ashlyn, Jilly had done it all and rejoiced in the time spent with his little girl and him. She'd been the annoying little sister he'd always wanted. He'd been the annoying big brother she'd never wanted. Amery always said she loved them both because he and Jilly were the same damn person. The only difference was he had a penis. To which Jilly would say, 'I have a penis some nights.'

Shit, he hadn't realized how much he missed her.

She stood at attention, which accentuated the way her white trench coat hugged her breasts, narrow waist, and full hips. The moment her eyes lit on the girls, Jillian's thick lips spread across her straight teeth—except for her upper right canine. A surprised chuckle rumbled in his belly, thinking about how much hell he'd given her over the years about that cute little tooth.

Ashlyn and Aria crashed into Jilly's trouser-covered legs, causing her to teeter on the skinny heels of her boots. Her infectious laugh, too often masked in sarcasm, jolted through his truck into his chest. He killed the engine, grabbed the girls' coats, and climbed out.

"Hey girls, be careful with her." The cold smacked his face as he headed for the trio.

Jillian's smile faltered. She straightened from hugging the girls and patted them on their heads. The closer he moved, the farther she backed away. Her index finger pointed at him accusingly. "Your dad has your coats."

Interesting.

Right after the accident, they'd spent nearly every waking, non-working hour together, consoling the girls and staying afloat. As time passed, her visits grew farther and farther apart and her excuses for not coming around multiplied.

"It's good to see you, Jilly." The girls ran to his feet. He purposefully held Jillian's gaze, measuring her reaction, while he helped each girl wiggle into her coat.

"Yeah, well..." She shoved both hands into her pockets and shifted like the guilty party she was. "Work has been crazy." Her shoulders bobbed. "Lots of workshops, but you know, it's better that than people getting themselves blown to bits."

He let his hiked gaze fall to the girls and then rise back to hers. Lipstick chewed lips sank into her mouth for another round of biting. She sighed and then offered the girls her hands. "All right, girlies, you ready?"

As was tradition, his daughters placed their little hands in Jillian's and the ladies headed through the maze of graves to Amery's headstone. Callum did as expected, hanging back—but not daring to lean on Jilly's offensive brand of truck—to give them time. They called it girl talk, and honestly, he was afraid to know what they gabbed about.

This time, though, it seemed like she used it as an excuse to run away from him. Maybe she ran toward Amery—her best friend, her family.

One girl on either side of her, Jilly stood stiff and stilted as if she didn't know how to act in her own body. Knowing her as long as he had, he'd never seen her act so unsure. She'd always been the type to run full tilt into a room of strangers, arms wide, ready for anything. She had ferreted out each of their life stories before she left with no more than a stiff drink and a laugh.

Callum folded his arms against his chest. This was the first time he and the girls had been to the grave in two months. It was normal and right to move on. They didn't need to visit his wife's grave every day to remember her.

This was the first time he didn't want to visit. He wasn't forgetting Amery. He thought about her, not as often as he used to, but he talked to her about big decisions in the girls' lives. With each passing day and the finality of her death, his connection to her faded. Maybe it was just young love or rushed love, which tended to happen with a baby on the way. Maybe it was the time spent apart on missions, or perhaps, he was just a cold-hearted bastard.

Ashlyn's sobs reached through his musings. Callum straightened and found the more stalwart of his two children crumpled on the ground in front of her mother's tombstone. He took one step but stalled. Jilly melted to the grass and pulled Ashlyn into her arms like she used to, as she should. Aria, not one for being left out, cranked out her own sobs and clung to Jilly's white coat. The woman enfolded her into the knot of little limbs and frilly pink cotton and bound them together as a unit.

She hugged them as fiercely as he'd ever seen. Moments later, her own sob lifted on the breeze and filleted him wide. The need to comfort his girls overwhelmed him.

Whoa. Jillian wasn't his girl. Then why'd he think *his girls*?

He'd known Jilly for nearly eight years, and she fell under the umbrella of his aggressively protective nature. If she hadn't beat him to the literal punch, he'd have dealt with her scumbag fiancé—what was it—three years ago. Until today, the stubborn woman never seemed to need a shoulder to cry on or arms to hold her together. So sure, she was one of his girls.

Instinct carried him up the slight incline and past the all-too-familiar graves. He saluted Amery's headstone and then knelt. His arms spread wide and secured three weeping bodies. Only Jillian's met his chest and crotch.

Christ. Here he was, in front of his wife's grave, holding her best friend and his girls and noticing the way her lush, firm curves pressed against his junk.

Callum focused on Aria's scrunched, red face and the deep sobs that wracked Jillian's frame. He didn't rock or soothe them; he just held them together, held them to him, and found solace in their warm, living bodies.

Jilly's fingers sank into his forearms, clinging through the material. Soon, the hands slid to the backs of his hands and hugged them against his daughters' heads. Her face burrowed into the crook of his arm for a blissfully long moment that stopped his heart and scrambled his brains. Too soon, she straightened and tamed her tears. She planted fat kisses on the girls' heads who still wept in her arms.

"Girls," Jilly whispered. They ignored her attempts to soothe and shush them, too far gone into their misery.

There was only one thing to do when the girls were too far gone in any emotion to pay attention. He sang, or rather barked, a cadence song from his days in BUDS.

"A hostage situation,
It started in Iran.
And then the bloody Russians,
Invade Afghanistan."

Aria's head perked. "HEY!" She'd added the punctuation with more gusto before, but he'd take it.

"Men at war-oooooor,
Men at war-oooooor," Ashlyn chimed.

"Late at night when your sleeping, UDTs come a creeping," he continued.

"All around-oooooound, A creeping all around, HEY!" They both joined in and continued to the next verse without him. Each line grew more boisterous than the last until they became a graveyard spectacle.

When they hit the line about the enemy finding their leader dead, Jillian jabbed him in the ribs. She tossed a glare over her shoulder. "And you gave me grief about saying blown to bits?"

"Somebody has to give you a hard time." Probably not the best choice of words but old habits and all. Usually, when he delivered the line, he added a suggestive brow waggle. This time, since his hard time was wedged against her ass and they were atop his wife's dirt-covered coffin, he kept his eyebrows still.

Jilly freed his chanting girls. He stood and offered her a hand up. Like always, she stood on her own two feet. Unlike always, she took a large step back.

Her heel caught the edge of Amery's tombstone. Both her arms flew back, and she careened backward over the granite slab and toward the ground. Aria and Ashlyn screamed. He lunged and caught Jillian around the waist. His hands fit too damn well in the sloping crook.

She scrambled off the side of the slab and out of his arms like he was a straight-up perv. And wasn't he?

"Are you okay, Jilly Billy?" Ashlyn ran to her side.

"Daddy catched me from falling too." Aria hiked a thumb at her chest.

"Caught," he corrected.

"Yeah, he caughted me." Her prideful smile was too big for him to bother with correcting her again.

"Come on, girls." Jilly reached for their hands and rushed toward the trucks. "I'll buckle you in tight."

"Are we going to the beach now?" Aria stared up at her with wide eyes. "Daddy said we could go to the beach. You, me, Ashy, and him."

From a yard back, he couldn't see Jillian's face. He didn't need to. Her rigid posture returned. When she reached the truck, her boot heels struck the asphalt with deafening blows, even at his distance. He hung back and watched as she buckled Ashlyn into the rear passenger side and hugged her tightly enough that it seemed like a goodbye.

She scooped Aria into her arms, rounded the tailgate—away from where he stood at the grill—and repeated the ritual. He walked on the silent feet he used for murder and blocked her retreat with his frame.

Jillian turned and jumped as if she weren't a highly trained and combat-proven soldier. "God, Callum. Make some noise, would you?"

"Nope." He grinned. "It'll get me 86'd."

"Daddy, what does 86'd mean?" Ashlyn asked.

"It means you don't need to know." He lifted his gaze to his daughter for one second, and Jilly slipped under his arm and dipped around the open door. He winked at his girls, closed them in the warmth, and followed the woman he thought he knew but was beginning to understand less and less.

"What's your deal, Jilly?" he barked.

"My deal?" Her long loose hair fanned wide as she spun in a short angry tornado. "I thought your new gig was safer."

"It is. I'm not leaving the girls, but I can't lose my touch."

She backed toward her door.

"You still didn't answer my question," he reminded.

"I don't have a deal. I'm cold and tired."

"You're acting like you don't know me—like we haven't laughed the hours away over a bag of potato chips and a beer, like I haven't carried your drunk ass in from my back lawn and held your hair back when you puked on my carpet, like—"

"I get it." When she got angry, her upper lip curled into a sneer, revealing her little crooked tooth.

"Whether you're acting weird as shit or not, I know you. I've never known you to shirk from confrontation. So nut up." Again, maybe not the best choice of words. He hated how different things were now that Amery was gone. Things he'd said to her a thousand times before never seemed crude or inappropriate until today.

"You told the girls we'd go to the beach together?"

"I told them we'd see. Besides, what's the big deal if we did? Amery wouldn't want us to never go to the beach again because she's dead."

"Us? You and me? You don't see anything wrong with that?"

"Just because Amery is gone, I'm not going to get weird on you, Jilly." He hoped, at least.

She braced both hands on her hips and puffed out her chest. He'd said something wrong, and he didn't have a damn clue what it was or how to make it better.

"The girls would love to see you more. They need stability. We need you in our lives like..."

"Like before?" One severe brown brow arched.

"Yeah."

"Well, I need…" Her lips pressed together, rubbing off the last of her lipstick.

"What do you need, Jilly?"

Her anger fell away. Hollow eyes welled with sadness. "I need distance."

"From the girls?"

"No." Her head shook.

"From what, then?"

"From you."

He knew the words were coming. They still hurt like a motherfucking knife to the guts. "Why?"

"Have you gone through Amery's things?"

He should have kept his mouth shut. Jillian had gone through everything with the girls, boxed up what they wanted to keep, donated a lot, and boxed up things that he needed to go through. He hid the boxes at the back of the closet and went on about his life.

"I'll text you with my new schedule. I've signed on with a private outfit for some trial runs."

"You retired from the Navy?" he croaked.

"You're not Navy anymore, Base Branch." She used the name of his employer like a curse word.

"Yeah, but I told you before I did it."

Jillian opened the door. "You wouldn't have approved." She climbed into the cab, slammed the door, and left him all alone with his dead wife and precious girls.

Chapter Three

Four months later...

Jillian squeezed her wide hips through a long ago abandoned cook chimney. If Callum were here, his big hands could press her ass cheeks together and wedge her into the space, which was exactly why she was here and he wasn't. Rock and dirt scraped her cheek as she dropped the ten or so feet into the old adobe section of the aggregate complex. Damn dirt floor didn't give and the impact stung all the way to her brain stem. She gritted and rolled toward the corner. The barrel of her AR-15 scanned under an old cot. No tangos.

"In position," she whispered in the comms link.

"Let's move," Colby Winters ordered in her ear.

She crouched at the door and counted down. Three. Two. One.

Rocco's we're-here-to-fuck-up-your-night explosion shook the building. Bits of dirt and debris rained from above. Lights flickered. Jillian blinked a chunk from her eyelashes and reached for the solid wood door, ready to move down the hallway to point B.

A blast of heat enveloped her and tore the door from its rusty hinges. Red and black clouds tossed her into the far wall as if she weighed less than Amery did. The impact thieved her breath. Garbled voices hollered into the earpiece, but she couldn't hear them over the sharp ringing of her eardrums. Talk about permanent hearing loss, which wouldn't matter if she died today.

Jillian's heart rate spiked. Now, she knew what it took to clear her mind of Callum and the girls. All she could think about was not dying. Distance from Callum's sculpted arms and the memory of how amazing they felt wrapped around her had been the goal. Death had not.

Another blast shook the foundation. This time, farther away.

"Fuck," she growled.

Again, noise cracked in her comms.

"Can't hear shit except the ringing, but I'm alive." She shoved the door off and scrambled to her feet. Dust fogged the doorway.

A shake of the head and waggle of the jaw restored a healthy buzz.

"Fall back," Winters barked. "They rigged this place to hell, and we're fucked in here."

"You're saying we retreat?" someone shot back.

"No, asshole. I'm saying draw them out and pick 'em off. I'm saying don't get blown up."

"What's going on?" Jared Westin demanded.

"They have the place rigged." Winters growled tactical maneuvers to Cash and Roman. "Cooper, can you climb out?"

Jillian scanned the room. The cot and low cooktop put her three or more feet from the ceiling. "Negative."

"Hold your position. If you see any unfriendlies, eliminate them," Winters directed.

"Roger that." She pressed her shoulder against the doorframe and waited.

The pop-pop-pop of high-velocity rounds stung the night air. She blocked the noise and the incessant ringing and strained for the slightest sounds beyond her point. Shouts echoed from distant corridors. Footfalls thundered in the opposite direction. Seconds turned to minutes.

"Cooper, you sure it's in the central room?" Winters growled. "That's a hell of a way to go with this many hostiles."

"That's not what I said." Jillian shook her head. "Your intel pointed us here."

"Intel I'm beginning to think was thinner than their reported number of soldiers." Jared snarled into the remote link.

"I said the energy pull is coming from that room. If they have the warhead, they need a cool place to keep it. But that pull could originate from a large computer or a tanning bed, for all I know."

Laughter filtered past the rapid fire of large rounds.

"A tanning bed. Hilarious." Roman cackled. "I'm getting a tan outside at three a.m."

The desert would do that to a man or woman in the dead of night and even inside. Dry, relentless heat stifled every breath.

"Thinning out on my end," Cash announced.

"Still shit over here," Rocco gritted.

"Silent over here. Permission to move?" Jillian nodded, willing the answer she sought.

"Affirmative. I'm headed to point B. Don't shoot me," Winters said.

"And have Mia lock me in a strait jacket in a padded room for the rest of my days? I'd never." Jillian moved slowly, methodically down the hallway. More quietly than a ghost, she cleared rooms one at a time, moving closer to the heart of danger.

If the stolen nuclear warhead they'd been tracking for the last forty-eight hours was here, they'd have more than a sleeping night's watchman guarding the thing. Unlike the last four rooms she'd cleared, the next one's door stood wide open. A tingle of apprehension crawled up her spine. One inch at a time, she peered and then eased into the room.

A dark, dirt-covered hand clamped around the barrel of her rifle and shoved it away. The move pushed her back to the corner. White teeth and wide, angry eyes appeared from behind the door, crowding her. Words flew from his lips too quickly for her to decipher.

Infidel and *die* registered.

Jillian palmed her K-Bar and aimed for the temple. One clean strike. The man went down in a heap. A quick scan showed an empty bunkroom. She retrieved her knife, gagged on bile, and sheathed the tool.

She could do it. It didn't mean she had to like it. Wires and timers were her thing. Time to find one, a big one. Back in the hallway, she took a right and braced for the firing squad she expected outside the door. The corridor remained eerily deserted.

This was the room shown on the schematic. Her heart beat in her forehead and her pulse screamed in her ears. After two months of clearing IEDs from Middle Eastern town's friendly to the Titan Group, she'd gotten the break she'd wanted. No, the break she'd needed—a full-time gig on the other side of the world. This was her chance to prove her worth to Titan and the world.

"At the room." In the open, Jillian placed her back against the wall and craned left to right.

A body fell from the mouth of another hallway into hers.

"Ditto." Winters eased around the corner and jerked his head toward the door. "Check it. I've got your six."

Jillian searched for trip wires and sensors but found none, not even a proper door lock. She shook her head.

"Me high. You low." Winters held up his index finger and then middle. On three, he thrust the bottom of his boot just above the knob.

The door splintered and swung wide.

From behind the desk, a man lunged for his gun. Jillian fired. One shot. One kill. Winters took out the two-man security detail, standing with their rifles across their chests.

They moved as a unit into the room, checking left and right.

A massive computer and its cooling towers lined one wall.

Disappointment used her lower intestines as dental floss. "Damn it."

"No warhead," Winters relayed into the comms. "We have a mainframe that's going to give you wet dreams, Parker."

"Hook me in and let me be the judge of that," Parker Black chided.

Jillian stowed her irritation for later and moved to guard the doorway better than the chumps who'd been inside it. Winters moved to the console. His fingers pecked across the keys.

"Perimeter secure," Cash reported.

"Interior almost secure." Roman's grunts, the smacks of fists meeting flesh, and a satisfied sigh fed into the line. "Secure."

"Hold the building. It'll take me a few minutes to see what we have," Parker ordered. "But yeah, it looks like a world of fun for Lexi and me."

***

Safely back at Titan's Middle Eastern headquarters—the Abu Dhabi hotel she now called home—Jillian marched into the war room. She slumped into the first open chair she found. Thank goodness, it was close to the door. If Tucker railed her too hard for the fuck-up, she could duck and run.

"Hiya, doll."

Jillian peeled her chin from her chest and sought the owner of the Australian accent. The quintessential Bondi Beach heartthrob flashed her a wicked smile. She'd never seen the man in the war room or around the hotel. A quick scan showed several more new, smokin' hot faces around the table. Australia's bedroom eyes sizzled effortlessly but revealed more than the good Aussie probably ever realized. The come-here-and-let-me-roast-off-your-panties vibe defiantly hid something more intriguing, not that a hottie roasting off her panties wasn't appealing. Too damn bad he was the wrong hot guy.

"My name is Ryder." He leaned in and offered his hand and a wink.

"I'll bet it is." She eyed his hand as if it was a steel trap ready to take off her hand at the wrist.

His grin bloomed. "You're a saucy one, you. What's your name?"

"Cooper." Jillian offered him a quick, no-nonsense handshake.

"Well, that name doesn't suit you at all. It's a boy's name, and you're a stunning creature." His gaze raked her top to bottom. "Made just as a woman should be."

"Cooper matches me and my balls just fine."
She gave him the universal suck-it gesture with two
hands smacked sideways to the crotch.

"Maybe you'll show me later?" The corner of
his mouth quirked, but the other half faltered
enough to let her know she was getting to him.
Most women probably fell to this guy's feet, but
boy, had he picked the wrong one to mess with and
on the worst day. Her damn ears still rang.

"Only if you let me shove them down your
throat." She stared at him with a world-record
deadpan expression.

A steamy Latino whistled across the table,
pointed at Ryder, and said something in
Portuguese. She really needed to brush up on her
languages. Beside him, a pure-bred American hunk
chuckled, while the man next to him whooped.

"Delta team, I'd like you to meet, Jillian
Cooper." Winters sat at one end of the table and
nodded toward her. "She's our EOD. Don't fuck
with her. She'll blow you to pieces with a bomb
made from the shit under your bathroom sink."

The entire room guffawed.

"Cooper, these are the feral creatures we call
Delta. This old bastard next to me is their fearless—
or psychotic—leader, Brock Gamble." Winters
chucked the man on the shoulder.

"Cooper." Gamble touched a finger to his
brow. "Looks like you fit in around here perfectly."

"That's the best compliment I've ever had,
sir." Jillian tipped her hat to him.

"So, Jillian, are you seeing anyone?" Ryder
leaned in again.

Jared strode into the room. Operatives, Titan
and Delta alike, shut the hell up and followed his
progress to the head of the table opposite Winters.

"Eyes on the screens, everybody." He looked at Parker, who sat behind a laptop clicking and typing furiously. "Here's what we know. Last night's mission wasn't a total loss. Parker pulled off some useful intel. We're waiting for a few more pieces to fit into place. As soon as we have confirmation on those, we move together. Two units but in sync."

He pointed at the first screenshot of a topographical map. "This is Al Hajar. You were two clicks off the mountain at today's compound led by Talha Nassar, now deceased. His cousins, Sassoman and Jassim, own respective compounds here and here on two sides of the Green Mountain separated by one click. Also, Talha's buyer has an outpost in Muscat. Judging by the intel we—and by we, I mean Parker—translated from the millions of encrypted data files, one of these three have the warhead. Or, most likely, are now trying to move it to a new location, since Talha has been compromised."

Jared cracked his knuckles and let his gaze meet each soldier in the room. "I don't have to explain to you how important it is that we secure the missing warhead. But I will—"

"Motherfucker." Parker growled the curse word and typed three times as fast as he had a minute ago.

Everyone's gaze swung to the cool and collected ass-kicking computer genius. In the short time she'd been around the central team that comprised Titan, she'd never once heard or seen the man's frustration. If Parker was ruffled, it was something big.

"What is it?" Jared demanded.

"Hacked. We're getting fucking hacked." Sweat collect on Parker's brow. He threw off his headset and leaned closer to the screen.

"Not possible. Your system is impenetrable," Cash scoffed.

"Look." Rocco pointed at the screen.

The information they'd been neck deep in had vanished. In its place, her picture and personnel file with more classified information than should be seen by even the highest levels of the intelligence community appeared as boldly as the sun on a desert day.

"Why is that up there?" Jillian's lips went numb, muffling her words. A cold sweat collected at her nape and charged down her spine.

"Cut the main line." Parker continued typing frantically.

"We'll lose our intel." Jared's chest puffed, and his jaw bunched.

"If we don't cut the main line, we won't have anything." Sweat slipped down Parker's nose onto his computer. "Someone else will have it. Your information. Your family's information."

Jared lunged for the main line and yanked it out of the wall with both hands. Several guys around the table jumped up to help. The line ripped through sheetrock up to the ceiling. Rocco, the closest, scrambled forward with a multi-tool and severed the line.

Parker's typing didn't let up a fraction.

"Is it offline?" Jared bellowed.

"Yes." Parker shook his head.

"Why the fuck are you shaking your head and saying, 'yes.' Either it is, or it isn't." Jared stalked to Parker's side.

Jillian couldn't breathe. Her picture still clung to the flat screen.

"I'm backtracking to find out who the fuck did this, what they were after, and what they got." Parker snarled at Jared. "Give me a fucking minute, okay? Yes, this is your organization and our intel, but this is my baby. Somebody just molested my airtight, doomsday prepped baby."

Everyone took a step back or sat with loud thuds. No one said a word.

"If we cut the main line, how are you still online?" Jared asked.

"Mobile hotspot, Boss Man. I don't have time to explain further." Parker typed and cussed under his breath, and Jared took another step back.

Jillian swallowed past the lump in her throat but still no air filled her lungs. Next to her, the hair on Ryder's arms stood on end. Around the room, everyone watched Parker's every keystroke as if it were the last twenty seconds of the closest game the Super Bowl had ever seen.

"No way." Parker sighed and canted his head.

"What, for the love of all the fucks, Parker?" Jared scrubbed a hand over his face.

"What you see is what they were after." Parker Black pointed at the one lit screen with her face on it. "And you're never going to guess where the hack came from." He reclined in his chair.

"Christ, Parker. We're not guessing. Spill it already," Winters barked. Jared released his white-knuckled grip on the back of his chair and shook his fist at the computer genius.

"Base Branch's D.C. headquarters..." Parker tossed his hands up.

If the sky would part and swallow her whole, she would go willingly.

Parker continued, "...by a douchebag with the screen name SEAL the Deal."

Jillian fumbled for her heart, but the slippery bastard glided right through her fingers and onto the floor. She buried her head in her hands and waited for the inevitable.

"I'm guessing you can answer a few questions for us," Jared said.

"Oh, fuck," she whispered. Years of battle and bomb construction and disassembly—shit, not even junior high—could have prepared her for the embarrassment burning her cheeks. "He's a friendly," she mumbled from cover.

"Doesn't seem friendly, hacking into my baby like that," Parker growled.

Jillian shoved the hair from her face and straightened to face the firing squad. They all stared at her, awaiting an explanation.

"It's my fault. If only I had called him and let him know where I was..." She couldn't finish the sentence.

"Why didn't you?" Jared asked.

"He's the reason I'm on the other side of the world." Jillian shrugged.

"Has he hurt you?" the steamy Latino growled.

"No," she snapped. "Callum would never hurt me."

"Hmmm." Winters popped a handful of Dots into his mouth, grinned, and chewed.

"What, hmmm?" she snapped.

"Little Jilly's on the lam." Cash chuckled.

"On the lam from love," Winters finished.

"Screw you both. It's not like that." Jillian crossed her arms over her chest, huffed, and slammed against the back of her seat.

"Yeah." Jared's lips pursed. "We've had more than a few of our own on the run from love. It's never like that until it is." He shrugged a stalwart shoulder and then turned to Parker. "How long until we're up and running again?"

"Ten, fifteen minutes." Parker swiped at the sweat on his brow and turned to Jillian. "Friendly or not, I need to talk to this guy. No one has ever hacked my baby, and I need to know exactly how he did it. I needed to know yesterday so I can keep it from ever happening again."

"I'm sure Cooper will be more than happy to pick up the phone and get her old friend over here ASAP." Jared smiled and lifted two palms in surrender. "Kidding. I have an old friend in Base Branch who'll scare some sense into this guy."

"He doesn't scare easily." Jillian couldn't keep her mouth shut. After a reprieve like that, she should. If Parker only needed him for security purposes, maybe she could get out of seeing Callum at all.

Jared simply smirked. "In the meantime, everyone pack your gear and be ready to roll in one hour. We have a nuclear warhead to retrieve."

Chapter Four

Callum glared at the screen, willing the words to change. They refused to bend.

Abu Dhabi.

Jillian's D.C. condo was occupied by a middle-aged woman with three kids and an obese cat because she'd sold it to move to the middle of the God-forsaken desert on the other side of the world.

He clamped his hands together and dropped them to the tops of his legs. Inside him, rage swirled in tight circles, juggling swords and flaming batons. Try as he might to shove them aside and focus on no more than the inhale and exhale of the next breaths, sharp and sizzling edges gored deep. The lances hit healing flesh, tearing it into gaping lacerations.

Cord Strong shoved through the front door with two steaming cups and a small paper bag clamped between his teeth. He stopped short in the foyer and removed the bag, pinching it between his index finger and a cup. "Bruh, I talk you out of your fury—as silent as it might be—dip out for less than five, only to return to your insane form of non-violent, violent temper tantrum. What the hell?"

If Callum moved right now, he'd tear his house apart from foundation to rafters. Palms together, he focused on the one thing that brought him solace. The girls' precious faces refocused his mind's eye. Only this time, rage for their loss amplified his own.

"It worked once, so let's rehash for posterity. She asked for distance, you gave it to her, and now, she's MIA." Cord continued into the living room and set a cup on the coffee table next to the cursed computer.

Why were they rehashing? Over the last four months, he'd done it in his head a million and one times.

"Why'd you give her the space to run?"

That was a new question—one he didn't want to answer to himself, much less out loud, even if Cord was his good friend and hacker mentor.

His friend kicked back opposite the TV as if it was actually on and streaming the History Channel.

"What was I supposed to do?" Callum clenched his hands together until his forearms shook.

"Tell her how you feel." The blond billionaire, Green Beret, and computer genius on loan from his family's company, Stronghold Technologies, shrugged like dropping a bomb as devastating as Hiroshima wasn't a big deal.

"Right." Callum turned and paced a line in front of a wall of shelves filled with knickknacks, books, and pictures. "Hey Jilly, I know the sight of us causes you severe pain and heartache, but the girls really need you. So stow it and continue showing up."

"For a smart son of a bitch, you really are dense sometimes." Cord smacked his cup onto the table with a thud. "I taught you how to hack like a pro in a month. You led a goddamned SEAL team through the Afghan mountains and captured Alab Sharik. Put something with boobs in front of you and game over."

"Keep talking and we'll take this conversation to the yard," Callum growled. He had a feeling he knew where this conversation was headed, and it spiked and bottomed out his heart rate in near equal measure.

"Think about it." Cord tore into the bag, extricated a round, sugar-covered, fried piece of dough, and popped it into his mouth. He held up another and waggled it at Callum with a questioning brow.

"For the thousandth time, no."

"More for me." His friend shoved another heart stopper down the hatch with a smile. "Right after the accident, she hung around a lot."

Callum pinched his forehead. She'd done more than hang around. Jillian had taken care of his girls and the arrangements until he'd gotten back from what would be his last mission with DEVGRU. Even after he'd been back, she'd cared for them all, like she belonged...there...with them.

His jaw hinged wide.

"Now, you're starting to think." Cord used a donut hole to gesture at his head before he tossed it back. "Things were getting..."

"Comfortable," Callum supplied.

"She was getting comfortable with her best friend's family. Not a great place to be when the people you love will never be your own."

Cord's words hit him like a herd of Spanish bulls. Each nuance bruised and gored a new inch of skin.

"That's why she moved to Abu Dhabi." The words burned their way up his throat.

"I thought you didn't know where the hell she was. That's why you were steaming." Cord crumpled the empty bag and swooshed it into the basket of remote controls on the coffee table. "What'd you do?"

"You know what I did." Callum shoved off the couch and stormed to the window. Outside, everything looked as it had for the last four years. His wife died, and the birds still chirped. Jillian ran away, and the sun still rose.

"She's the kind of girl who'll lop off your manhood for hacking her personal information."

"What do you think Titan will do?"

"No way."

Callum rested his forearms against the frame and stared at the matching pink and blue bikes he'd told the girls to put away before they went to the Stronghold Estate to spend the day with their Aunt Milly. The woman wasn't blood, but she'd been a nanny to Cord and all his crazy siblings. Ashlyn and Aria loved her, and Milly had saved his hide on more than one occasion.

"No fucking way." Cord sprang from the couch and cleared the room in hungry strides. "How did you do it? I've tried, for shits and giggles, and failed every time."

"It was..."

The front of a blacked out SUV almost kissed the pavement, skidding to a stop in front of the house. Callum's hand flew to his sidearm, and he stepped to the edge of the window.

"Boobs are not going to be the death of me." Cord retreated to the door and pulled his own pistol.

"Donuts are." Callum strained to see through the thick tint. Nothing.

"Real funny, Dick. Maybe you should've thought more and hacked less. I swear, I teach you right from wrong, but it slipped right through your dense skull."

"One door." He expected every door and hatch to ooze combatants. Only the driver's door opened and slammed closed.

"This guy is about to have a really bad day." Cord chuckled.

Dark hair with gray sideburns peeked over the top of the vehicle. Vail Tucker's boots pounded across the lawn, catching the walkway halfway to the door.

"Yes, I am." Callum holstered his weapon and nodded at Cord, who opened the door in time for the Base Branch Director to stomp across the threshold.

Premature gray clashed with the man's brawn and the usual agility and grace with which he moved. Today, authority and attitude kept in check by years of experience in war zones and special operations roiled at the surface. It bubbled and popped in his eyes, and the beat of his pulse that thundered at the base of his thick neck.

"I can appreciate you sacrificing the danger—leaving a job you love—to ensure the best you can that your girls won't be alone in this world." Tucker braced his hands on his hips and pinched. "With a baby of my own on the way and a stepdaughter who means the world to me, I understand it a hell of a lot. What I can't comprehend is risking your life for a broad."

"She's no broad." His cool-under-fire exterior cracked. Callum's chest rumbled with vehemence.

"Who is she then?" Tucker demanded.

Christ, he was trying to figure that shit out himself. Callum thought he knew, but now... "She's complicated."

"It'd better get uncomplicated A-the fuck-S-A-P. You hacked Titan, which means you hacked me. Do you know what happened to the last guy to turn traitor? I visit him once a year on the anniversary to make sure he's fed enough, not too hot or cold, and is provided enough medical treatment to live." Tucker nodded. "I make sure aspect is optimum for him to live every day in misery. Next time I visit, I'll bring you with me."

"I only skimmed personal documents until I found what I needed." Callum hated the excuse coming out of his mouth, but he hadn't breached their security with malice.

"How would you feel if someone hacked our system and skimmed our personal documents with your address, where your girls live?" Tucker's accusing finger swung to Cord. "What about your known relatives and associates? You have quite a few."

"That's enough." Callum took a step toward the director.

"What did you mean by you hacked Titan, you hacked me?" Cord ignored Tucker's jibes and Callum's outburst and worked the situation like his half-soldier, half-hacker mind always did.

"I mean before Jared Westin was known as boss man, I knew him as a comrade. His blood is my blood. His goals are my goals. His men are my men. I protect them as such." Tucker sucked up the distance between them. "Does it make your blood stir? Does it make you want to squeeze the life out of whoever breached your security, security never before breached?" Tucker's eyes darkened.

Hell, yes. He hadn't thought about it from any other perspective before he acted, which was so out of character for him. Why the fuck had he done it?

"I needed to know she was okay." He rubbed a hand over his face and drew his first full breath since learning Jillian worked for Titan on the other side of the world.

"You're going to get the chance to see for yourself. You're wheels up in thirty." Tucker pushed an index finger into the center of his chest. Callum held his ground. With the words attached to that finger, it proved tricky.

"To Abu Dhabi? To Titan?" Cord's arms shot wide in a WTF.

Tucker kept his eyes trained on Callum. "It's time to stop tiptoeing around this shit called life. Your girls don't just need you to be alive. They need you to live. Titan cut their main line because of you. The least you can do is go show them how you got in so they can close and bar the door."

"I have to see that." Cord rocked on his heels and chewed on his knuckle.

"No." Tucker didn't think or blink.

"But I taught Cal the tricks he used to get there. The least you can do is—"

"No." The director finally broke his gaze and turned on Cord. "Parker Black doesn't want you within a thousand miles of his equipment. After we figure out what this genius did, you have to make sure no one can do it on our system. Plus, if you're the all-powerful teacher, Strong, why didn't you teach this numbnuts who not to hack?" Tucker didn't wait for an answer, only pinned Callum with the no-nonsense gaze. "Get ready. I'm driving."

His thoughts immediately flew to Jilly and then the girls. "Have Milly watch the—"

"They'll be fine." Cord waved him off. "Go. Don't be stupid."

Chapter Five

"That's good, Rocco." Jillian smacked the edge of her fist on the extended cab's roof just in case. She blew a dirt-caked flyaway from her eye.

The tailgate stopped centimeters from the concrete loading dock at the hotel's secure basement entrance. Roc, Cash, Winters, and Roman poured from the vehicle. Delta hung back, checking the perimeter of a CIA on steroids level secured facility. The team stood at the dock with itchy fingers and dancing toes. Just like that, she realized they awaited her instructions.

Pride lifted her from the sorrow plaguing her since the uproar with Callum's security breach. As nice and equally dude-ish as they were with her, she'd never be part of their team. She didn't save the world like they did. She dismantled bombs. Maybe one day, she could have a team of her own— an elite EOD squad that she trained and ran.

"Okay gentlemen, this is the most important piece of luggage you'll ever carry. One bump and we're dust, along with about two point five million people. Forget your kids, lovers, and loved ones for the next ten minutes. They don't exist. This warhead is your world. Treat it as such."

Finding the thing packed and ready for transport saved them time on their exit, but it also meant the nuclear material was exposed to the heat longer. She assigned each man a corner and waited for him to reach his position.

"On my three. One. Two. Three." Jillian orchestrated the lift with both dirt-laced hands and then gestured at the building. "We have to get it to the cooler without dropping it. If you need to rotate out, holler." They scoffed. "Do not let your egos get us vaporized. If the shit gets heavy, say so."

A round of hooahs, oorahs, and hooyahs echoed off the concrete and steel. The men followed her methodical march down the corridor, through the security doors, and into a cooler large enough to fit a tank. Sweat dripped from their brows and noses. Their muscles held steady.

"Center the foam and lower slowly on my three. One. Two. Three." When the hunk of metal and extremely hazardous material met the platform without incident, Jillian sighed.

The men erupted into silent celebration. Good. They respected the monster, as they should.

"Okay, Cooper." Winters pointed at the warhead. "Do your thing."

"It has to cool for at least two hours before I can safely dismantle it." She shrugged. "And that's only if we get this door closed right now."

"Everybody out." Winters called out to the team, but everyone had already made his way out of the cooler and away from the warhead. A few feet wouldn't save them. They followed and locked down the basement.

"I'm not going to lie. I won't breathe right until you work your magic on that thing," Cash announced.

"Me either," Jared barked in their earpieces. "Get cleaned up. Debrief in the war room in one hour."

A string of yes sirs littered the air. Everyone hit the elevators. She peeled off from the group on the floor below the main team. Just another way of saying she wasn't permanent. Alone in the corridor, Jillian felt her skin prickle. Titan was bringing in Callum to walk Parker through the breach and try to scare him into never doing it again. She didn't know whether he'd come and gone, was still here, or hadn't yet reached Abu Dhabi. Not knowing if it would hurt her more to see him while he was here amped her nerves. The eerily quiet corridor didn't help, either. Of course, it was almost four a.m., and any sane person would be curled up in bed.

Jillian unlocked her door while banking a yawn. No time for sleep but a shower...oh, yes. She used her body weight to heave the thing open and dropped her ruck of EOD tools just inside the door.

A hand wrapped around her extended wrist and yanked her inside the room. Already off balance, she stumbled into the danger zone. Her right hand reached for her sidearm. Unyielding muscle blocked her elbow, limiting her mobility. The slamming door echoed loudly in her brain. Closed in with the enemy.

Panic kicked its feet on the dash and reclined in the passenger seat. Training steered while skill shifted and rage stomped on the gas pedal. Jillian tucked and rolled, wrenching her hand out of the grip. That had been the goal, anyway. But she looked at the hand. The tattoo wrapping its way up the heavily veined arm had taken top billing in more than one of her dreams.

"Callum?"

His other hand bit into her shoulder, and he spun her to face him. Alarm bells and wailing sirens sang between her ears. Run. Run away now.

"Never enter a room with such inattention."
Callum pulled her to his chest so hard she should
have bounced off and fallen to the floor. One thick
arm around her back held her close.

The audacity of his actions bolstered her
outrage. "The hotel is safe or didn't your hacking
show you the amount of security in place here?"

Callum's rough palm scraped its way up her
waist. Jillian's heart stuttered. This was a dream.
She had to have fallen asleep on the ride to base
because this couldn't be real. Real or not, his
fingers entwined in her hair and yanked her gaze to
his. Middle of the desert at midnight eyes stared
back as they had a thousand times before, but
something inside them shifted, ignited. Her chest
ceased all function.

He lowered his forehead. All the sand and
filth from her body jumped inside Jillian's gaping
mouth. Speaking and swallowing were no longer
options. His forehead pressed against hers.

"Safety is an illusion, Jillian. You should
know that."

She knew it, which was why she'd put
distance between them. With him this close, she
couldn't afford to think about anything other than
the reason he was here. Jillian drew on her anger.

"I knew you were behind the breach, even
before they knew who'd done it. Are you trying to
get me fired?"

"If you'd only answered my calls."

"You're not responsible for me, Callum. I
don't have to answer your calls or answer to you."
God, she was such a bitch. If she made him angry
enough, maybe he'd leave her to wallow in her own
misery.

"No." His thumb pressed against the point of
her chin, holding her captive. "You don't have to

answer to me, but I needed to know you were okay. Whether you like it or not, you are mine to protect."

His concern pierced deeper than his anger. Jillian closed her eyes, willing away tears that sprang to the surface. If only she were his, but he belonged to another, to someone she loved more than she loved herself.

Hot, soft lips pressed against hers. His dark, masculine scent shot up her nose like an illicit drug. A moan seeped between her clamped jaw. Tears streamed across her cheeks. It wasn't a dream because her dreams satisfied her hunger, made her tingle, and freed her. This taunted, hurt, and imprisoned her.

"No." Jillian planted both hands on his chest. A majestic landscape of plateaued muscles snuggled under a well-fitting T-shirt mocked her. She shoved hard.

Callum released her face and widened the gap between them but didn't let her go. His eyes narrowed. The one-inch scar below his left eye wrinkled with his concern. "Do you blame me for not protecting her? For not being there when it happened?"

"No." None of this made sense. She didn't blame him for anything...except being too hot and caring, hard-assed, and amazing at everything.

"If I could have traded places with her, I would have. I was the one with the dangerous job. I was the one we preplanned a funeral for."

"I know," she whispered.

"Do you? Every day, I see the hurt on my children's faces. It kills me. Then they lose you too."

Anger exploded behind her eyes, leaving her momentarily blinded. Jillian closed the gap and pointed a sharp finger at his sternum.

"They haven't lost me. I video chat with them nearly every day. I've never forgotten a birthday, Valentine's Day, Memorial Day, Halloween, Thanksgiving, or Christmas in their entire lives. I'm not about to start."

Three solid raps on the door caught her off guard. "Jillian?" Roman called from the other side of the door.

"Fine." Callum pulled her close again. One hand circled her waist while the other sank into her shoulder. "I lost you, and it pisses me off."

Jillian swallowed so hard she nearly choked on her tongue.

Callum's jaw flexed. His gaze remained locked on hers. "And now you're trying to get yourself killed."

"It should've been me." Tears, unwelcome and stored up for too long, streamed down her cheeks.

"What?" he growled so forcefully, the reverberations careened through his fingertips, pierced her tactical clothing, and radiated through her.

"I didn't have kids. I didn't have a husband. Hell, no relationships to speak of except for your family. Amery's family." The fissures of Jillian's heart cracked wide again.

"The three of us made our own family because our blood abandoned us. It didn't belong to one of us any more than it did the other." His hold became more of a hug. It hurt and healed in almost equal measure.

Almost.

"She was the linchpin, the heart that held everything together." Jillian slapped at her tears. Another knock sounded at the door, but it seemed so far away. "Come on, don't tell me you never wondered why it couldn't have been me. Then your family would still be together."

"No!" His bellow filled the room.

"You should."

"No!" His head shook so hard it might break a vertebra.

"Yes." Jillian planted her hand to push him away again.

Callum barred her forearms to his torso. His other hand clamped the back of her neck and yanked her in. His mouth landed on hers with barely hinged force. His lips and tongue slid over her mouth, demanding her participation.

Her brain yelled, 'Stop.' Her body said, 'Shut the fuck up.' The two sides played tug-of-war with her heart.

Callum kissed with his entire body. His hand caressed. Hips undulated. His body cocooned her. But Jillian didn't give herself permission to engage. Her fingers robbed her of the decision, curling around the collar of his shirt and holding on for dear life.

"Jesus, Jilly."

Her nickname groaned between their melded lips jerked her from the depths of desire and exposed her to the harsh sunlight. Callum wasn't hers to covet, much less kiss. She turned her head in time to see the door swing wide and Roman Hart push through with his pistol trained on Callum.

"No." Jillian twisted and placed herself between Roman and Callum. Just as quickly, she was whirled around and shielded by a back twice as wide as her hips. "He's Base Branch Operative Callum Bradfield." She lunged from behind him.

"Sweetheart, that's reason enough to shoot him." Roman winked and holstered his sidearm.

"Damn it, Jillian." Callum turned on her. "If you ever throw yourself in front of me, I'm going to —"

"What? Spank me and put me in the corner?" She snarled at him like the confused and feral creature she was, like the creature he created. Before him, before the dreams, he'd been just her friend and her best friend's hot husband, and she'd been sane.

"Tempting." His whisper coiled around her spine and spiraled her thoughts in too many devious directions.

"All right, you two break it up." Roman stopped near the beveled entryway mirror and pointed at Jillian. "You, clean up and be ready for briefing in forty." His finger swung to Callum. "And you, asshole. Jared's been looking for you for almost as long."

"Exaggerate much? I've been gone for ten minutes, and I told him what he needed," Callum explained.

"He wants you close while Parker works through it. Find him where you lost him. I'm going to shower off the desert. If I have to track you down again, I'll shoot." Roman's brown eyes matched his dirt-caked face perfectly and narrowed in warning before he turned and walked out, leaving the door open wide.

Callum drew a breath to speak, but she held up a hand. A very dirty hand.

"Go. I'll be in the war room in thirty."

His jaw waggled.

"Sure you won't run away again?"

"I didn't run away."

"Yeah, you did, but I'm a good tracker." He touched the tip of her nose, turned, and left, closing the door behind him.

Chapter Six

One by one, in small groups, operatives filed into the war room and took their seats around a large conference table. Each time the door opened, Callum's newfound anxiety scaled higher. Sure, his briefs bunched, waiting to see if Jillian would show. Even more than that, the number of warriors piled into one room unnerved him.

"What's going on?" Callum asked the boss man.

Jared Westin stood over Parker Black's shoulder and snarled like a rabid dog, but the computer whiz seemed impervious to it. Neither his fingers nor his eyes deviated from his task—track down the source of the original breach.

"Don't worry about it," Westin barked.

"I don't know much about Titan, but I know it's a privately held company. I know you don't have hundreds of teams like Branch. The UN backs Base Branch, which means several hundred countries. Most of your guys are in this room, which means something big is going down. Normally, I wouldn't care about it, but you have Jillian square in the middle of this shit." He crossed his arms and gave as good as he got.

"First off." Westin reached his full height. Callum had him by several inches, but he would never look down on a man with such grit and hard-earned legend behind his name. "I don't have her here. She's a grown-ass woman, who came on her own skill and accord. Second, I like you. You're perceptive and well trained. Third, this is bigger than you and Jillian, and even your dead wife."

Instead of getting angry—which he could easily do—Callum focused on the message Westin smacked in his face. Without a single detail, he told him exactly what was at stake here. Everything.

The hairs on the back of his neck stood on end.

"The lady of the hour," someone said behind him.

Callum turned and watched Jillian rush to a seat nearest the door, farthest from him. She plopped her lush ass into the chair so quickly he couldn't fully appreciate the way her knee-high black boots, maroon pants, sheer white blouse, and mini leather jacket hugged all her angles. A damn shame.

"Your magic hands ready for the job?" A guy he knew as Ryder waggled blond brows.

He stood so closely to the Aussie, he could probably snap his neck before anyone tried to stop him.

"One more hour." Jillian stared at her fingertips, fingertips that toyed with treachery every day.

"I found it." Parker Black's deep blue eyes nearly bugged out of his head. "It was cloaked on my end, which is why I never saw it to begin with. Jesus Christ. Someone cracked the door long before Bradfield."

"He was just too proud to realize he'd gotten luckier than the most elite hackers in the world and dumb enough to waltz right in," Roman quipped.

"Thank fuck." Parker pointed an accusing finger at the screen. "Otherwise, I'd have never known it was there. This thing is beautiful and terrifying in its simplicity, mirroring its surroundings without revealing its presence."

"Who put it there and when?" Jared pinched the back of his neck in a crushing grip.

"It's going to take time, but I can follow the crumbs," Parker answered.

"We don't have time." Jared glared at his watch. "We have fifty-five more minutes until..." He slid his gaze to Callum. Jared scissored his jaw for half a second, and then continued, "...until Cooper can dismantle the warhead."

Holy shit. They were sitting on a nuke. He'd heard one had been stolen out of a Russian facility. He'd thought it was better off out of Putin's hands. Callum should have known better. Anyone dumb enough to steal from a Russian was worse.

"I want eyes on it now," Jared ordered.

"But sir, if we raise the temperature—" Jillian shot forward in her chair.

"If it's not there, you can't disarm it at all." Jared pointed around the room. "Titan, make sure it's there and that it stays there until Cooper can dismantle it. Delta, hit the lobby and bar and get a read on the hotel. Anything that looks suspect, you have my permission to get to the bottom of it."

"I can help." Callum spoke only for Jared's ears.

"You can hinder too," Jared shot back.

"I won't. I have girls to get home to," he explained.

"And another one to take with you when you leave?" The boss man shrugged innocently.

"She's a grown-ass woman." Callum gruffed. "I suppose it'll be up to her."

"Titan, make room for Bradfield. Unattached Delta, don't make goo-goo eyes at Cooper or Bradfield will try his damnedest to pop them out of your skulls."

Jillian—the hard-ass who never blushed—turned the shade of an Atlantic sunrise.

"Bloody hell, all the hot ones are claimed." Ryder shoved through the door.

"Let's move." Winters swept the room with his arm and followed Delta.

Jilly's blush turned into a scowl he knew he'd pay for later. He just stared back at the woman he'd known only two months shorter than he'd known his wife, almost as deeply but never as intimately. He'd always known she was beautiful. Why had he never noticed how his pulse raced when he looked at her?

Because he hadn't let himself. He'd been faithful to Amery until death parted them.

He beat feet behind the others down the corridor to a private elevator. Delta continued through a set of double doors toward their temporary quarters. No one spoke on the elevator as thoughts of security breaches and big kabooms quieted their minds. At least, they did his until he slid a glance to Jillian. She stole her gaze away and stared at the numbers blipping past on the readout above the doors.

They opened on B2. Callum bet no one else had access to or even knew a second level of the basement existed. Titan and Jillian rushed out of the elevator and down a brightly lit hallway. Callum took his time, scanning the perimeter for security sensors and cameras. The place was rigged better than the exterior of most bank vaults. No way could anyone steal anything from here without setting off alarms, causing lockdowns, and probably being scanned for facial recognition and biometric data.

When he reached the group—each person input a series of numbers into a keypad and then scanned their retinas for entry into the vault—he had no doubt the warhead would be chillin' where they left it. Jillian rocked back and forth on her feet, none too patiently awaiting her turn. She must have mistyped the numbers the first time because she cussed, shook out her right hand, and then pounded the keypad once more. After she thrust her face at the scanner, the red light above turned green.

A great whoosh that sounded like a spaceship airlock releasing created a funnel. It screamed past them into the crack between the large receding metal doors until the gap grew to more than an inch. The noise quieted to a low rumble of the cooling pump's engine.

Reacting to the heat rolling in from the corridor, a dense fog rose in curled clouds and spilled through the doors. The moment they were wide enough, Jillian slipped through. Winters tried to follow, but the width of the opening wouldn't allow him through. He and the others jockeyed and pranced for their go at the door. Finally, it opened adequately, and they piled into the room.

Callum had never seen men so eager to cram into a room with a nuke. He checked his package, nodded, and joined them...in the empty room.

Jillian's hands braced her forehead as though her brains might pop out the front of her skull. She stared blankly at the open space where the warhead should be.

Each true-blue member of Titan blinked at the space, but slowly, one by one, their narrowed gazes lifted to Jillian.

"No." Callum strode forward two steps and turned on the team.

"Callum, what are…" She pulled around his arm to glare at him, but the silently accusing team caught her attention. Her breath caught. The realization that suspicion fell on her played fifty emotions across her face until resolve straightened her shoulders. "No."

The solid word spoken with such conviction filled him with pride.

"Goddammit. The only way to prove I didn't do it is to find out who did." Jillian's voice was strong and no-nonsense, but her cheeks flushed red-hot. She was pissed, which ratcheted his own anger.

"There's another way." Callum took a half step in front of her. "I beat the notion out of them."

The tension in the vacuum doubled, raising the temperature of the cooler twenty degrees.

"You could try." Cash Garrison stepped forward with his fists loose but ready. Roman perked up at Cash's back.

"Stop." Winters held up both hands and walked into the middle of the divide. "There's an enemy. They stole a nuclear warhead from under our noses, but it's not any of us."

"How can you be so sure? He hacks us, shows up here, and now, the nuke is gone." Cash snarled at Callum and then swung his gaze to Jillian. "And she deals in bombs. I don't think she stole it, but who's to say she didn't sell it to the highest bidder and use him as a cover."

"I say," Callum whispered the word, which brokered more menace.

"Look, Jared and Parker, guys who know a hell of a lot more than us vouched for them both."

Winters addressed his team and then eyed him. "Why'd you hack us?"

Callum didn't owe them a goddamned explanation. He could dole out a broken bone or two before being taken down by the team, but what would that help?

"If they know your motivation—" Winters started.

"I know I crossed a line. I'm sorry for putting your families in jeopardy or perceived jeopardy." Callum rubbed the knot at the back of his neck. "A part of my family was MIA, and I wasn't thinking clearly. Priority one was finding out where she was and making sure she was okay."

Besides him, Jillian didn't move or make a sound, but the murderous expressions on the guys' faces slowly eased to gratuitously violent.

Winters pointed at him and Jillian. "You two find out who betrayed us. We found the warhead once. We'll do it again."

Everyone filed out of the chiller, leaving him and Jillian literally in the cold.

"I'm out. Just like that." Jillian's face fell. Her gaze hit the floor like a rooftop jumper. Its sadness splattered all over his boots and rattled something loose inside him.

"It's not you—"

"What? It's not you, it's me?" She snorted. "I've heard that one before."

"No, smartass. It's them. They're a tight-knit group who've been working together for years. You're the new face. When shit goes down really close to home, you look at the things that stand out, and you do."

Callum eased toward her. God, did she stand out. Her sullen eyes that always had so much spark begged him to reignite their fire. Her curves made his palms itch.

"What the fuck am I supposed to do now, sit and wait?" Jillian's palms slapped her thighs. The sound shot through him, right to the tip of his cock.

Until a few weeks ago, he'd never sexualized her, but now that he had, there was no stopping him. Every glance, every snarky comment, every move did crazy things to his body, and sent his mind on a tactical reconnaissance of what-ifs. What if he ran his hand up her muscled thigh? What if he jerked her pants down her legs and spread her legs wide? What if he and Jilly worked together as more than friends?

"You have a new mission. We have a new mission." He meant it in more ways than one. "Look at me. Show me you hear exactly what I'm saying, Jillian."

Dark eyes that mirrored his own lifted. Callum interlaced his fingers with her right hand. A possessiveness—that had nothing to do with her job, his girls, or devotion to his dead wife's friend—called to him like the roar of a wild beast to its mate. He lowered his head to hers, not to test the waters or gage her reaction. His lips pressed to hers for the pure awe and delight elicited by the meeting of their two mouths.

Unlike before, Jillian yielded to the first touch of his lips to hers. She opened and received his tongue. A long sweeping taste told him all he needed to know.

If she couldn't get past Amery's ghost, he was fucking screwed.

Callum cupped her cheek with his free hand and dove in for seconds. Her tongue tangled with his, hungry and involved. Panted breaths sighed over his lips. Her fingernails bit into his palm. He pulled her closer. The intensity of their exchange revved his long dormant yearning to new life.

Jilly's lips tore from his mouth, and Callum blinked the world back into focus.

"You can't keep kissing me." Her words said he really shouldn't do it, but her quiet moan and swollen pupils centered on his lips contradicted them.

"Once will never be enough."

"It has to be. We can't do this again."

"Why not?" he asked, out of breath enough that embarrassment crept its way up his cheeks. Hell, as sexual experience went, she probably outdid him. Amery hadn't been his first, but she'd been his second and only for a long time. They'd met as little more than children, ready to serve their country.

No way would he let inexperience or his dead wife scare him away. There wasn't a faster learner than Callum Bradfield was, and he was more than ready to learn a trick or two with this fiery woman.

"It's not right," Jillian whispered.

His hands dropped to her thighs. The hard curved flesh hidden by tight maroon pants fit perfectly in his palms. He lifted her into his arms and backed her to the wall. The heavy ridge of his dick nestled against the junction of her thighs. Her breath caught and jaw slackened.

"Tell me that doesn't feel right." He started a slow push, rolling his hips forward. His imprisoned cock stroked her clit from tip to root.

Jillian bit wine-stained lips that matched her pants, as though willing herself not to react. She studied his intricate tattoos as her balled hands hovered over his forearms.

"Put your hands on me, Jillian. Feel me."

Her hands flattened and lowered. The touch connected them and electrified everything. She pulled him close. He obliged, leaning into her, while reversing his hips until their most intimate parts no longer touched. The dull edges of Jillian's fingernails bit into his arms, and a satisfied rumble purred from his chest. He exhaled against her neck and nipped a line to her earlobe.

"Do you feel me?" His teeth ran the crest of her jaw to her lips. When she didn't respond, he stilled completely. "Jillian, do you want me to stop? You can walk away now, and I'll never put my hands on you again."

She gripped his arms so hard the blood stopped flowing. Her inhale shook them both. Callum swallowed the saliva pooling in his mouth as he waited and prayed.

"I should." The edge of her forehead dropped to the side of his cheek.

Callum's chest cracked wide. The soft, pliant skin of Jillian's lips kissed his cheek. It was a wartime goodbye, an I-may-never-see-you-again-but-you'll-be-in-my-every-thought farewell lovers shared before being ripped apart.

Only they never had the chance to be lovers, yet he loved her all the same. He knew it by the pain of his fragile heart being torn from his chest. He'd known it by the blood trail she'd leave as she walked away from what they could have been.

Jillian laid another heart-wrenching kiss a fraction of an inch closer to his mouth, and then another closer still, until her lips hovered over his.

"But I can't." Her lips bumped into his as she formed the words that salved his open wounds.

He held still, needing her to make the next move.

They shared several shaky breaths. Callum looked into her eyes, seeing Jillian for the first time as she was—haunted and yearning and more beautiful than he ever realized. Her lips quivered as the soft, textured skin caught the upper edge of his. She pulled his lip, urging him to open for her. His mouth parted and Jillian toyed with it, dragging hers across, dropping them low, and tugging his lower lip into her wet heat.

His hips drove the tempo higher than before. He drew her knees above his hips and pressed them toward the wall. She rewarded him with frantic pulls on his tongue. The pointed tips of her nipples pushed against the silk of her bra and the sheer fabric of her blouse, meeting the unrelenting push of his chest.

"Callum." Jillian mumbled his name against his lips. Breaths rushed in and out of her mouth at a delirious pace. Her hips rocked in time with his.

She felt so good, so wild and on the verge of everything he wanted to give her, many times over.

One step at a time.

Her kisses grew fewer and farther between. Rasped heaves and tiny sighs poured from her lips. Jillian's eyes clamped shut. She shook her head in a slow back and forth, fighting it.

"I know what you need." Callum pinned her face to the wall with his forehead. He deviously slowed his thrusts. "Come, Jillian. Come for me."

Her hands slipped up to his shoulders. She pulled him in and circled her hips. "Yes."

Good Lord, her willing surrender spiked his own need, but this wasn't about him. The angles of his attack varied with each plunge.

"Oh, yes. You know what I need. How? I don't... Oh, yes. Yes." She whispered her

tumultuous orgasm to the world and no one at all.
It was spectacular.

Slowly, the vibrant red he'd coaxed into her
cheeks eased. Her breaths slowed.

Callum braced himself for a Jilly tirade. She
could give the best he'd ever seen. He'd pushed her
past her comfort zone into new, terrifying, and
delicious territory. She didn't like things she
couldn't easily categorize.

Jillian buried her face against his neck. A
cold trickle weaved its way down his neck, and then
another.

Man, he hadn't prepared for tears, but they
endeared her to him all the more. Callum wrapped
her legs and arms around him and exchanged their
places. The cold metal wall stung his back. He
hugged Jillian to him. Her leather jacket squeaked
under his hold.

He rocked back and forth and smoothed her
hair behind her ears. She started the headshake
again.

"Don't do that. We're doing nothing wrong."

The woman he knew well straightened with a
spark in her eyes. Her swollen lips pressed together
through another torrent of tears. "I am."

"How?"

She opened her mouth, closed it, and then bit
her lips. Her gaze hit the ceiling as Callum waited
for her to find the words. He needed to know why
she thought this was wrong so he could find a way
to show her it wasn't.

Her head canted and eyes narrowed. "Look."

For a few seconds, he thought it was an intro
into her gentle letdown. When she didn't elaborate,
he followed her line of sight to the fan grating
twelve feet up at the top of the chiller. A small

rectangle of paper, a wrapper maybe, lay flat against the wide mesh.

"Okay?"

"This is a clean space." She wiped at her tears and scrambled from his arms.

"So?" Shit, he'd never felt colder in his life. He liked her warm curves against him, a lot.

"I made sure it was clean before we found the warhead, and I know that wasn't in here when I locked it up two hours ago." Jillian grabbed at the small seams of the large metal plates.

"You planning to use your spider skills to scale the wall?"

She faced him and planted both hands on her hips. A hint of a smile curved her red mouth. He wanted to kiss her again.

"Get over here and give me a boost then." Her smile dropped off, and pure Jilly attitude challenged him to try something and lose a tooth.

Callum adjusted his pants. Jillian's gaze trained on his junk. Proving again what he had minutes ago. She wanted him—liked him—even though she didn't want to.

"Keep staring at my crotch like that and I'll give you more than a boost."

She averted her gaze to the paper. One step forward, two steps back.

He walked right to her and bent forward, leveling his eyes with her full breasts that peeked out of the kick-ass jacket blouse combo, and cupped one hand into a stirrup. "Up you go."

After eyeing him for a long second, she placed her boot in his palm. Her fingers gripped the back of his neck, and she placed the other boot on his shoulder. It gave him a perfect view of her crotch. He licked his lips and replayed one of those what-ifs in his head.

"Now who's staring at whose crotch?" She grabbed his extended hand and climbed, placing her other boot on his free shoulder so she stood fully on his shoulders.

"I'm staring, but I don't limit myself to your crotch." From the bottom looking up, her ass popped like a Christmas cherry.

"Men." She snarled. "It's all about the ass." Jillian snagged the paper between her fingers and shimmied down his front.

Callum locked his arms around her waist and stared into her eyes. "I'm not those guys, Jillian."

"I know." Her throat bobbed.

"I like this view more than all the others."

Her eyes closed.

"Eyes on me and listen closely." Callum waited until her lids parted. "This view gives me a clue into what you're thinking about. You're thinking about me. Crazy or unexpected as it is, I like it. I like it a lot." He kissed her nose and set her on her feet. "What'd you find?"

Jillian stared at him for several seconds before remembering she held one hell of an old-fashioned clue, considering the cameras and security system had been compromised. She turned the paper over in her hand, and her eyes bloated.

"It's the bypass code, written on an order form for the hotel restaurant." She shook the paper. "Only restaurant management has access to it."

"Why would they leave it behind?"

"I don't think they meant to, but you saw the current created when opening that door, especially when the fans are running. Maybe it slipped out of their hand, and they didn't have time to retrieve it, or it fell out of their pocket. I don't know, exactly."

"Well..." Callum smiled.

"Well, what?" Jillian hurried him with quick flaps of her hands.

"Looks like I'm taking you on a date tonight, and there's nothing you can do to stop me."

Chapter Seven

If she didn't touch Callum again, she could walk away and only feel like half a traitor. Right?

Who was she kidding? Jillian had labeled herself a traitor by lunchtime the day of the first dream, when the images of Callum thrusting deep inside her refused to wash away with the passing hours of daylight.

Jillian gazed out the wall of windows at the colors the setting sun painted on the blue waterfront. She should be surveilling the restaurant for an opening, so they could slip into the back without drawing attention to themselves. The problem was every time she turned her eyes into the room, they immediately sought the object of her many dreams.

"You look stunning." Callum drew her in with a perfectly fitting comment. Sitting across the dimly lit table from him—a warrior decked out in a suit and tie—was a turn of events she struggled to process.

"I am stunned," she quipped.

Jared had wanted them to look inconspicuous in the five-star establishment. The guy hadn't a clue the level of restraint he asked of her.

"Why?"

"Why do you have to ask such simple yet astonishingly complex questions?"

"Part of my charm." He shrugged, refilled her half-drunk glass of wine, and gulped his water.

"Are you trying to get me drunk? It's bad for business. Remember, that's why we're here," she whispered.

"Is it?" Callum's smirk unbuttoned something inside her. It had come out to play so rarely in the last year.

"Yes." She took a too-heavy sip from her goblet.

"I don't buy it." He lifted a hand before she could retort and continued. "I want to know why you ran halfway across the globe."

His dark suit matched his dark eyes and urged her to tell all. He had that effect on her. Anything he wanted, she wanted to give him, and she wasn't that kind of girl. Military life excluded, men didn't order her around. Never had. Never would.

Her palms dampened as she remembered his commands. 'Eyes on me. Feel me. Come for me.'

Jillian drew a stilted breath. "She was my friend, and I looked at her husband and saw something I wanted."

Goodness, but the truth—if only half of it—leaving her lungs made the next breath easier than the million before it. He reached across the table, but she couldn't let him touch her. When he touched her, she forgot the reasons they couldn't be together, the reasons why they'd never work.

"She was my wife, and I look at her friend, and I see something I want."

Her heart thundered in her ears. Callum's gaze held steadily, his jaw taut. "We're not doing anything wrong. I'll continue to tell you that until you believe it. Amery was in our lives, and we were loyal to her. She's not in our lives anymore."

And that was the crux of it.

"What would have happened if she hadn't died that day?" Jillian hated the question because she couldn't change what had happened. She'd tried every way she knew how—crying, begging, hoping, and praying.

"You would have continued to be her friend and I her husband. You would have found a douchebag—less douchy than Trent was—and you'd have married him and made me an uncle."

That never would have happened, not after the dreams. Tears she'd banished for the rest of the day welled to the surface. Screw stealth and a romantic dinner. Jillian had to get away before she embarrassed herself to the point of no return. She slid from the chair, grabbed a handful of black lace, hiked it, and ran.

Her strappy black stilettos beat a frantic staccato through the sea of linens and lights and a finery in which she didn't belong. High-browed eyes followed her escape with irritated sneers and scoffs. She ignored them, rounded the last table, and aimed for the dark hallway past the white fountain with a rearing horse. A server in a dark suit turned from the bar, gasped, and wobbled his silver tray of martinis atop a white gloved hand. Jillian smirked at him. At more than ten feet away, he wasn't in the slightest danger of being mowed over.

Something wet and bony hit her bare shoulder. It spun her like a fun fair ride. Jillian's arms shot out for balance, and her fingers sank into hot, damp fabric. Nearly one hundred eighty degrees later, she planted her feet on the slick marble floor and stared into the wide, brown eyes and a face obscured by a full, long beard.

Heat gathered in her cheeks.

"I'm so sorry." Jillian righted the hunched man and released her death grip on his white coat. The double-breasted front of the sous chef's top was tinted yellow with sweat and soaked through to his narrow shoulders. "I should have been watching where I was..."

She was about to beg his forgiveness and keep running because nothing added salt to exposed emotions quite like a mid-escape collision. The amount of perspiration sliding down his mocha face jerked her attention by the shirt collar. Sure, kitchens were hot, but this kitchen was a modern masterpiece. Sure, the pressure to perform could be great, but the night was slow.

"Titan." The man's wide eyes swelled larger still.

Before her mind computed all the variables, his arm shot out. A thin flat palm connected with her shoulder. On any other floor and in any other shoes, Jillian would have rolled through the sissy shove and pounced on him. Since she wore a dress she rented and shoes she'd bought that afternoon to impress a man who didn't belong to her, the hit pitched her backward. Her arms flailed once again in search of something on which to cling. She had nothing and no one in this world. The life she had known died with Amery.

The sous chef sprinted toward the kitchen while Jillian's ass and shoulder met marble with an unsophisticated smack. Air absconded her lungs. She fought through the panic that rode the coattails of every severe blow, and missile locked her gaze on the black double doors the man shoved through. Her hands found the cold, unforgiving surface. She pushed to her knees. Ornamentation on her ridiculous shoes tangled in the long lace and pulled her back to the ground.

Gasps and tiny feminine shrieks erupted in the dining area. A server shouted after the man but made no effort to chase him nor help her up.

Hot, measuring hands braced her ribs.

"Let's go." Callum set her on her feet and took off.

Jillian found traction on the balls of her shoes. She followed massive jacket-clad shoulders, a fine butt, and long legs across the room and through the double doors. Dishes and meals littered the floor in front of the delivery shelf. Flames rose from a searing pan on the stovetop where a chef flicked the contents with his wrist and bellowed over his shoulder at the chaos.

Callum powered past the mess, the line of slack-jawed sous chefs, a pantry, the massive metal door to the refrigerator, and turned down the first hallway. Steam rose from the industrial dishwasher where a man washing pots barely spared them a glance. Past the washing station, crates of fresh produce, and gigantic plastic bins of linens lined the far wall. Beyond him, Jillian couldn't see the man they chased, but she heard his frantic breaths and heavy footfalls in the distance.

A metal-on-metal shriek of hinges filled the corridor and then silence ensued—save for the rumble of the dishwasher. Callum hooked left into a loading area. Bins and grates stacked atop pallets filled the room. A forklift sat vacant next to an empty stack of pallets. On the far wall, a garage door took up residence next to a smaller one, but the likely door where their man fled was the nearest and worst option. The office trapped him perfectly.

"We don't want to hurt you. We're here to talk." Callum retrieved a pistol from the small of his back and motioned for her to stand down.

Of course, he would. Jillian glared, hiked her dress, and slipped the tiny revolver from her thigh holster. Callum's gaze burned her exposed legs. She dropped the curtain of fabric, smirked, and hurried him toward the door with a walk of her fingers.

When the man didn't respond, Callum stepped to the side, twisted the knob, and shoved the door wide. Pistol up, he eased through the doorway. Jillian's heartbeat raged in her ears. Callum Bradfield was the most competent man she knew, but even the best warriors died. He'd given up a job like this to ensure he'd be there for his girls. She shook it off. Sous chefs didn't carry guns. Knives maybe, but...

The guy hadn't bothered to lock the door?

Gooseflesh rolled a violent wave down Jillian's neck. She turned to see the edge of a metal pipe swinging hard and fast at her head. The impact knocked her out of her own body. The gong reverberated from far away. Instinct also caught the flight out of town. Her limbs refused to fight back. Hell, they refused to catch her as she tipped forward into the office. The floor met her fast, but she didn't feel the fall.

The sous chef kicked her legs inside the frame. She couldn't hear the door slam but saw it cut the light from the room. Maybe she lost consciousness. Maybe not. Callum hunched over her in an instant as he had so many times before... in her dreams. His rough hands roved her face and neck. His lips moved. Nothing translated, except his touch.

He yanked a landline off a desk and yelled into it. She still couldn't hear but could tell by the way the veins and muscles in his neck popped and flexed. Callum held the receiver away from his mouth, leaned over, and pressed a kiss to her forehead.

Sound screamed back to existence in a high-pitched whine that threatened to shatter her skull. Both hands flew to her head to keep it from splitting apart. Groans and inhuman noises interrupted the wail of her brain.

"I'm here, Jillian," he whispered.

"Get him," she growled.

"Something is blocking the door."

"He can't get away."

"I can't fit through the air vent, and even if I could, I wouldn't leave you." Callum brushed a strand of hair from her face.

"I'm fine." Her words sounded more like a moan than anything.

Callum yanked the mouthpiece in place. "Check the cameras in the fine dining kitchen, restaurant, lobby, and the back of the hotel. We chased a guy in a sous chef's uniform but lost him." He waited for a beat. "What do you mean the cameras aren't working? Never mind, the fucking hack." Callum's upper lip curled. "Tell them to hurry. If they catch him, I want the first crack at that asshole."

His gaze dropped to hers. Jillian willed the headache away, so she could better commit it to memory.

"I need a doctor to Jillian's room as fast as he can get there." Callum grimaced. "He clobbered her over the head and locked us in the restaurant's loading dock office. Thanks. We'll be waiting."

He replaced the receiver and pulled her more tightly to his chest. Jillian eased her forehead onto

his shoulder and exhaled the first full breath she'd
dared inhale.

"Jared's coming to bail us out."

"I don't need a doctor. I'll be fine."

"Stubbornness still intact, I see." Callum
smoothed his thumb over her brow.

"It's the only thing that's kept me sane for the
last year and a half." She offered him a weak smile,
but his narrowed gaze whipped it off her face.

"Year and a half?"

Jillian opened her mouth to correct the
number she'd given him, but maybe the slip was a
good one. If he knew everything...

Her stomach joined her head in the toss and
turn of misery. She didn't know how he'd react. She
knew how she should want him to—with revulsion
and pity to make her never look at him the same
way again—but she also knew it would hurt worse
than her head, worse than the dreams, worse than
Amery's death. And that was saying something.

"Before Amery died, you'd been gone three
months or so. Everything was perfect then, except
the girls—and even me—we missed you. Life was
normal. You came and went, I came and went, but
things were great. We were a non-traditional family
that did life. And then one night, I went to bed like
every other night. I took a shower, brushed my
teeth, and crawled into bed. I've been over that
night a hundred thousand times in my mind, nit-
picking everything, wondering if I'd done something
different would the outcome have been the same."

"Christ, Jilly, what happened?"

It hurt when he called her Jilly with her
content in his arms because he'd called her Jilly
before. It was how it should be, though.

"I dreamed...about you."

His lips pressed together, as though he forced himself not to interrogate.

"I dreamed of you over me, between my thighs, pushing inside me. I felt your hands on my hips and your mouth on my breasts, your arms around me, your breath on my face, and your words in my ear."

"It was just a dream, Jilly."

"That's what I told myself." She struggled to swallow past the emotion gathering in her throat. "I drank a cup of coffee and waited for it, for you, to fade into obscurity like every other dream. I drank the entire pot, washed and folded laundry, ran, and worked out, and ran again, trying to leave the feel of you behind, your smell, your touch."

She pushed away from him to sit, but his arms locked around her.

"And?"

"I stayed up that night, thinking that if I were smashed, then the next night I wouldn't dream about you. It didn't work. It was never the same dream twice. It wasn't every night. Those mornings were the worst because I had no excuse and still I woke thinking about you."

"Did you tell Amery?"

"No." Jillian shook her head. It pounded like a bass drum. "I hoped that if I ignored it, it would go away. I managed for a long time. Things were getting back to normal. Well, closer to normal, at least. You came back, and I didn't die on the spot. You left again. I'd made it—tamed my demon, if not conquered it. Then I got the call."

"My best friend, the center of the family I'd finally found for myself, was dead. For a fraction of a second, the tiniest part of me was happy." Fat tears slipped down Jillian's cheek onto her pretty lace rental. "I was happy because I thought I wouldn't feel so guilty obsessing over her husband."

A noise beyond the door robbed Jillian of the sobs building inside her chest.

"It's going to take me a minute," Jared called through the door.

Neither of them said a word as they heard metal and wooden crates tossed outside, emphasizing the silence in the small square room.

Callum's dark eyes hooded with thick brows. He held perfectly still like he did when he was pissed and didn't want to torch the world with his anger. The muscles in his jaw drew taut, as did the air between them.

"Say something," Jillian demanded.

For a desolate heap of seconds, he didn't move. The minute stretched to two.

Jillian rolled sideways out of his arms and flipped onto her stomach. The room tilted and shimmied beneath her palms. "Shit." Her stomach pitched back the first course. She hated puking more than she hated stitches or almost any other horrible thing in the world. The muscles in her neck contracted, refusing the package and returning it to the sender. A gag riddled the room.

"God, I hate when you do that. Just puke and get it over with." Callum braced her middle with his arm and pulled her hair from her face.

"No."

"Stubborn."

"We've been over that." She sucked in air through her nose and eased it through clamped lips. "It's what got us here to begin with, remember?"

"I know. I'm processing. It's just—"

The door opened. "Is she going to puke? If so, I can come back." Jared waffled in the doorway.

"She is not," Jillian assured herself as much as she did Jared.

"Good. The doc's going to be in your room any minute now." Jared stepped closer.

"I've got her." Callum lifted her off the floor and into the cradle of his arms. The urge to hurl hit her hard and fast. "Look at me." She did as he asked, unable to disappoint him even in her whirl of disgust. He didn't say anything more, but it was enough. The knot in her throat receded.

"I don't need a doctor," she insisted.

Callum's stony gaze flipped her stomach in a whole new way.

"I know what you need, Jillian."

Chapter Eight

"It's swelling to the outside, which means a nice fat goose egg for a couple of days. Your pupils are slightly dilated, and you lost consciousness." The fairly muscled and tall Indian doctor packed his stethoscope and thermometer into his bag as he spoke. "You have a mild concussion, but nothing to be overly concerned about as long as you take care for the next two to three weeks."

No more bumps to the head. Callum would see to that for her, a hell of a lot better than he had tonight. If the asshole had been wielding a knife or a gun, Jillian could have been... His fists ground into the mattress next to the woman who'd caught him completely off guard.

"I want someone waking you every two hours for the next eight. If there are any complications, here's my cell number." The doc extended the number to Callum.

"Yes, sir." He took the card, shoved it in his back pocket, and shook the man's hand. "Thank you."

"I'll see you out." Jared stepped into the open bedroom doorway and led the way through a small sitting area out the door.

"I've been awake for like two days already, and he wants my stolen hours of sleep interrupted,"

Jillian grumbled and elbowed the pillows, propping herself up on the headboard.

Jared returned to the room and assessed each of them with a measured gaze.

"I didn't have anything to do with the warhead's disappearance." Jillian sat forward. Her sharp gaze challenged boss man's right back.

"I know you didn't." Jared propped his shoulder on the doorframe. "I'm glad you two were in the restaurant tonight. The virus the hacker left killed the cameras, and the jackass got away, but based on your description, we have a narrowed field of suspects to sift through. We're cross-referencing all employees with links to the original thieves. Something will shake out soon."

"What have the teams turned up?" Callum hated waiting, even though he loved the woman he waited with.

"Nothing." Jared straightened. "This is the shittiest part, the wait, but you know."

"Yeah, we do," Callum agreed.

"Jillian." The boss nodded at the woman Callum was determined to make his, and turned to him. "Take care of her. As soon as we find this warhead, we'll need her skills."

He watched Jared retreat, heard the door click, and wondered if he could keep anyone he loved safe. He hadn't been able to protect Amery and dropped the ball with Jillian today. His girls. How were they? He knew they were safe with Stronghold but without him on the other side of the world.

Jillian wrestled a pillow from behind her.

"Two full days, no naps anywhere, huh?" Callum pulled her forward, removed two smaller pillows from the headboard, and eased her down onto the remaining one.

"None."

"Well, you have me beat for hours awake in a row."

"I know." A smile crooked the corner of her pretty red lips. "You can sleep anywhere; in the commotion of two toddlers or on a HELO about to drop into the mire of war."

"Remember the time I walked six blocks uphill in the rain because I fell asleep standing on the trolley in San Francisco?"

"I remember convincing Amery to leave you asleep on the trolley and you showing up at the hotel soaked through and pissed." A sweet chuckle shook Jillian's chest, drawing his gaze to her full breasts and the way the mounds pressed against the black lace bodice.

"You always were the little devil on her shoulder."

Jilly's smile faltered. "You always called me Little Devil."

"And you used to like it."

"I used to," she agreed.

"Amery needed you on her shoulder, in her ear, on her side. She was such an honest, loving, straight-laced person."

"She was perfect." Jillian sniffled.

"You know that's not true." Callum glared, grabbed her shoulders, and sat her in front of him.

The spitfire glared right back. "I know, but she—"

"She pleased others more than she did herself out of fear that they'd—we'd—abandon her like her family had. We were better than they were, and she still lived in fear."

"You were better than they were," she sneered.

"Goddamnit, Jillian. You broke nobody's vows." His fingers sank into her muscled shoulders. "Fantasy isn't in the contract, and even still, you didn't act on it. You were her friend, her best friend, and you loved her better than anyone in her life."

"Except you and the girls." Jillian argued with the best of them. She never quit, and he loved arguing with her.

"We required things of her. You required nothing. Amery feared abandonment so much, but you showed her how to live. If it hadn't been for you, she never would have experienced life out of fear for loss. When I called you Little Devil, it was out of praise and gratitude."

Her smile returned with a wicked slant. "Remember the time you fell asleep holding Amery's hand in the delivery room?"

"She was pissed." His grin matched hers. "As she should've been."

"The memories we share are everything, Callum."

"No." He shook her too hard, considering her head injury, but she didn't cower. She never would. "They're wonderful, special, but they are the past. Today is everything."

"Today is tomorrow's memories."

"What do you want tomorrow's memories to be?"

Chapter Nine

Callum pulled her so close, Jillian's breast smashed against his chest. Her head pounded with every frantic beat of her heart, but it faded into the background with all the doubt, all the reasons they couldn't be together, and all her guilt.

His heart thundered against hers. His dark eyes begged.

She knew exactly what she wanted. Only, she'd never been able to claim it. Here he was offering it up with no strings. Her throat stuck on the word.

You. I want you to be my tomorrow's memory.

"Jillian, it's only natural that people develop feelings they never anticipated for the people they love."

"What?" She choked on the question.

"I've loved you forever. You've been part of my family since we all realized we finally had one. Now, that's growing into something else, something more, and I can't explain it."

Her heart swelled and cracked clean down the middle into two pieces. He loved her. She had no doubt, but he only loved her because Amery was dead. No doubt she should get the hell over it because the best man she'd ever known wanted her. Could she ever move past that?

Callum tilted her chin up. "Can you explain how you had the fantasy of us *coming* together in your head for so long without acting on it? I've only played with the notion for a few weeks, and it's all I can do to keep my hands off you."

"Callum." His name morphed into a sigh.

"Kiss me, Jillian. Make a new memory with me. One memory and we'll see where it goes from there."

She might not be able to overcome all the obstacles between them, but she could make a memory. One tangible experience to replace the wisps and yearnings of her dreams.

Amery fell away.

Jillian's fingers slid up Callum's dress shirt. The silky fabric tickled the pads of her fingers until the feel of his unyielding muscle underneath burned the amusement away. Dark shading and the outlines of his massive tattoo bled through the white, adding the real level of danger to the primly dressed man.

She slipped her fingers under the loop of his tie and lifted her gaze to his. Darker than the night, his eyes bore back all the desire and emotion coursing through her at Mach speed. She held him so tightly that he couldn't get away, even if he'd wanted to.

"I'm not going anywhere, Little Devil." He whispered the last against her mouth, only inches from his. The steam of his exhale parted her lips.

Pride swelled along with need. It pooled in her belly and eased its way between her legs. Her clit pulsed, readying for the ride to come.

"I wouldn't let you go, not tonight." She pulled him down to her mouth.

Her red-stained lips pressed to his. Callum held perfectly still, no longer coaxing her participation but demanding it. He was hers to take if she had the balls to do it. Luckily, she'd been born with a pretty pink pussy—but she'd developed the balls through life's trials.

Jillian enveloped his lower lip in hers, clamped it between her teeth, and pulled him closer. She dragged her tongue across his soft skin, taunting. A small growl rumbled up his throat. Her throaty sigh reciprocated as she sucked his lip to the tip several times, wishing like hell it was his cock. This wasn't a damn dream. If she wanted something, all she had to do was take it. She released her hold on his mouth. Callum's hands held firmly at her back but allowed a hint of air between them.

One inch at a time, she coaxed the tie through the loop until the two ends parted. Callum's tongue slid across his swollen lip. Her insides quivered. The intensity of his gaze made every dream look like a worthless rendering of his features. He trained it on her, freeing something buried inside her soul, while she methodically unfastened each button on his shirt. Without pause, she continued to his belt buckle and zipper.

She lifted her hand to the sliver of Callum's skin peeking out from his shirt. The shaking of her hand stole her breath. She was the one with the big brass balls—the one always down to try something new—and recognized her fear for what it was...total and utter anxiety. This wasn't just some man she was undressing. This was Callum, the man she'd wanted for too long.

"No undershirt?" The stupid question would give her time to process and adjust.

Callum played no games. His passion held, as did his tongue.

Jillian gulped a breath, flattened her palm, and fused it to the center of Callum's chest. His skin warmed her hand, and the contact gathered force with each thump of his heart. She added another hand and slowly glided them over the smooth plane of his chest to the craggy tops of his shoulders and down his sculpted arms.

She unwrapped him like the most patient kid at Christmas, exploring every dip and rise, every texture and value. He was the prize, the one she'd treasure until her last breath. Only when her touch made him release his grip on her did his fingers slip from her back. His cuffed sleeves dropped, and the rest of his shirt followed onto the bed.

"I've seen you without a shirt a thousand times, but..." Emotion clogged her throat.

"You've never been the one to take it off me." Callum pressed his thumb to her chin. He dragged it down her windpipe and over her sternum to the V of her neckline and into her cleavage. "We're about to do a lot we've never done, and I'll enjoy every fucking minute."

Her lips parted on a gasp.

"Every sigh." Callum dipped his thumb behind the tapering lace strap and yanked it off one shoulder and then the other, exposing her breasts. Involuntarily, she gave him the sighs he sought.

"Every moan." He skated his knuckles over her chest and strummed them over the peak of one nipple. She clamped her lips together. Callum cupped her heavy breasts and molded them with hard, sure strokes. Jillian's head lolled. The moans rose into the air where they were meant to be.

She interlaced her fingers with his and shared in her own demise.

"You were undressing me, Jillian. No need to stop."

She pulled her legs under her and sat on her heels. They rubbed dangerously close to her throbbing clit, so she wiggled to get them where she wanted them.

"If you want me to undress you, you're going to have to stop touching me like that."

His gaze slid hotly over her body. "From where I'm sitting and watching your hips move, it looks like you're stealing my job."

"It's been my job for a long time," she panted.

As much as she hated him to stop touching her, Jillian pulled their hands from her breasts. She tossed his shirt to the floor, wrapped her hand around his scruffy jaw, and pushed. "I wanted to taste you in the back of my throat and all over my tongue."

"Jesus." He gripped two handfuls of sheets. Every strikingly developed muscle flexed in his arms and abs, across his shoulders, and dipped down to the open fly of his pants.

Jillian licked her lips, and he watched her work. Two fingers hooked into the band of his boxers. She pulled them back inch by inch. The broad, rich, pink head of his cock threatened to strike. A string of pre-cum dangled between his underwear and the dewy seam.

"Jesus is right. We're going to have to pray after this." Jillian gnawed on her lower lip and wrestled his pants and boxers over his big, fine ass and down his massive thighs. She didn't care what happened to them after they shoved over the edge of the bed. Callum's long, vein laden penis demanded her attention and her mouth.

Her fingers met silk at the base of his shaft and dragged across it to the plume of his head. She lifted it into the air and encircled the thick column. "Lots of prayers."

Their gazes met. She needed a signal that this was as earth-shatteringly amazing for him as it was for her, and the look in his eyes told her all she needed to know. When she leaned forward, her nipples grazed the rumpled sheets. She licked away the pooling moisture and rolled it around her tongue.

"You taste better than you did in my dream."

"I fuck better than I did in your dream too," he growled.

"Promises, promises." Her lips bumped into the wet crown as she spoke.

"Feeling is believing." Callum's fingers sank into the lace-covered flesh of her upturned ass cheek. The bite hinted at pain, but pleasure flowed lava hot across her skin.

"Yes, it is." Jillian licked her lips, opened wide, and swallowed him to the back of her throat.

"Fuck, Jillian." The sheets went taut in her periphery. Callum's grip wrenched them almost free from the sharply tucked corners. He stretched her throat so much, her eyes watered as though she were a first timer.

With him, she was.

She breathed through her nose, sealed her lips around him, pressed her tongue to his smooth length, and reveled in the feel of Callum. Her pace started slow and built. Each time his grip on her ass intensified, so too did her enthusiasm for loving him with her mouth. Slurps and pants clouded the air. A ferocious growl caught her off guard. Callum's hand left her ass and clamped the back of her neck. Sheer desire coursed through her, starting at the back of her throat and warming its way to every naughty bit she possessed.

Callum shouted his release into the room, loud enough that the concierge at the other end of the hallway probably heard it. Jillian liked his inhibition, loved it. He pulled her off his cock with the hand at the back of her neck and dragged her to face him. She licked her raw lips. The sting brought her as much joy as the coal fire burning in his eyes.

"I don't think you have to worry about sleeping at all tonight." He yanked her down and stole her breath with a kiss. His tongue sparred with hers. "I want to watch you come ten different ways, find the one you like the best, and then do it again."

"Yes," she begged.

"First, I have to get you out of this damn dress." Callum eased from under her. When she moved to sit back on her heels, he caught her hands and placed them on the bed.

Over her shoulder, she watched him stand, kick off his shoes and pants, and then turn back to the bed. His cock hung full between powerful legs. He hooked her hips and pulled her knees to the edge of the bed, flush with his thighs. The impact thrust a moan from her lips.

Callum's hands smoothed over the globes of her butt, rocking her back and forth with the circles until they skated up her back. He stopped at the low cut of the dress several inches above her crack and dragged the zipper down the short trail. When he pulled the dress from her body, the humid air full with the scent of sex caressed every inch. It pooled at her knees. He shimmied the fabric under her legs, and finally, she was free with him.

Her heart kicked and bucked, her muscles quaked, waiting for him to make his move. And wait, he made her. He assessed her from top to bottom and back again. Jillian shifted her gaze over her other shoulder, following his progress. His approving eyes and interest provided nearly all the progress she needed to come. One false move and she'd tumble over the edge and hit every orgasmic rock on the way down.

"My turn to taste." Callum dropped to his knees. His rough hands spread her knees wide and then her ass cheeks, exposing her.

He suctioned his mouth to her clit just as she'd done his lip, sucking to the tip again and again. Her hips jerked in turn with his frenzied rhythm.

"Oh, shit. Callum. Yes."

His fingers sank into her cheeks, and his mouth hovered over her, while his tongue dealt the final blows. She screamed the last of her orgasm in broken words and pleas.

"The dimples above your round ass are going to be the death of me." He playfully bit one cheek and shoved her onto her back.

Callum prowled up, kissing and exploring every inch of her with his mouth. He paid special attention to the shrapnel scars at her waist. Then he was there, over her, staring down as he had so many times before, but this was nothing like those times. The fear of him running away, calling her a devil, or her waking and losing him to the morning light drowned in his weight and determination.

"You, every part is going to be the death of me, and I welcome it with open eyes." She braced his face in her hands and pulled him to her mouth. He kept his eyes on her too and kissed her as sweetly as she'd ever been kissed, sweeter than a man of his size and ability should be able to.

His forehead rested atop hers, and his eyes required her attention.

"I'm here. I'm with you," she assured.

"I love you, Jillian, and I've fallen in love with you."

She loved him—had since the first week they'd met. She'd been in love with him for nearly as long. She just could never admit it.

The blunt head of his cock pressed at her opening.

"I'm on birth control."

"If you weren't, I wouldn't stop."

Hasn't history proven he didn't care about that little detail when pussy was on the line?

"Hey." He lifted her chin. "Trust me, Jillian. Be with me, here and now."

Jillian wrapped her legs and arms around him, exhaled through the ache of his intrusion, and held Callum inside her. The man filled her in every way. His rigid shaft stretched her tight walls. His love tore away the hurt and bitterness she'd held close for so long.

"Make love to me, Callum."

He rocked into her with slow, measured strokes. She strained, pulling him deeper each time, needing to take everything he offered. The rippled V of his abdomen massaged her slick, swollen clit. His hungry gaze drove her higher over the crest too soon. Her fingers sank into the muscles on his back. Her release cried from her lips. Breath panting in and out of her lungs, her orgasm hugged her tight and ricocheted her through the air where she collided with stars. She descended to the earth out of breath and disoriented but wanting Callum's release more than she wanted her own.

She drove the pace higher, circling and popping her hips.

"Not so fast." Large hands stalled her efforts. His own efforts persisted, slowly, methodically. "I have all night." His abs bunched and flexed as he glided in and out of her slick pussy. "And I plan to use it."

Callum rolled onto his back. He held her to his chest and took her along for the ride until he eased her back. Both his hands molded her breasts together and held them for his pleasure. His tongue flicked one nipple and then the other. His lips latched onto her left nipple and bit. He gripped her hips and moved her back and forth on his cock at a leisurely tempo destined to break her mind.

"Your curves are worth dying for."

"You're not allowed to die." She pulled his head higher, pressed her mounds together, and shoved his face in the pillowy softness. "Unless it's suffocating in here."

"What about suffocating between your legs?" His muffled words reached her, while he wallowed in her cleavage.

"That'll work too." She giggled.

He nipped at her breasts and then pulled her mouth to his. This kiss held a promise of the deviance yet to come. And come soon, if he wasn't careful. When he broke the kiss, he shoved her upright and gripped her thighs.

"Ride me like you've wanted to, Jillian. Don't hold back."

Sweet Jesus.

Jillian braced both hands on his pecs and leaned forward so that her breasts plumped toward him. She arched her back, loosened her hips, and put them to work, sliding up and down his shaft as if she'd been made for it. He thrust and pulled with her. The gorgeous dip of his hips just above his cock rubbed her sensitive nub. Her breaths grew shallower and closer together, matching Callum's.

"Just like that." His jaw locked, and his nostrils flared.

He came in a furious roar, spilling himself, hot and alive, inside her. Every beautifully etched muscle contracted, and his gaze remained locked on hers until their breaths evened.

Callum pulled her to him. He pressed her cheek to his chest, smoothed the hair from her face, and held her close. His erection remained nestled firmly inside her body. The soft touch of his lips pressed to her forehead.

"Eight more to go," he whispered.

Chapter Ten

Early morning light filtered into the wall of windows they hadn't spared a second to draw the curtains across. Jillian's backside nuzzled against his hip, while her head nestled in the crook of his arm. Her dark hair spilled across his chest instead of her arm. She lay like she wanted to be there, not like she had to be. After years of being Amery's crutch, being wanted beat being necessary by a mission's worth of clicks.

Callum rolled to his side and tucked Jillian into the shelter of his body. He shifted the strands of hair from her ear, delighting in the fiery red highlights the sunlight reflected in her dark hair. She smelled like him and sweat, causing his abused cock to stir.

"I thought you were kidding about the eleven." Jillian mumbled her words into the mattress. "Now that I know you were deviantly serious, there's no need to try to top it today. Forget the two-hour rule. I haven't gotten two hours all night. Go back to sleep."

He pressed a kiss to the hollow behind her ear and smiled against her neck. "I had to make the most of it. You seemed convinced once would be enough. I had to prove you wrong."

"Again?" Her arms and legs reached as far as they could. A yawn keened in the quiet room. She

rolled against his chest and buried her face
between his pecs.

"Yes."

Jillian's heavy sigh lifted her shoulders. Her
breath warmed the skin covering his heart. Slowly,
deliberately, she pressed her kiss-swollen lips over
his heart and owned him with the simple touch.
When she eased back, Callum braced the side of
her face in his hand. Her eyes closed, and she
leaned into him.

"I'm yours, more than I was ever Amery's." He
didn't whisper the words. None of their meaning
would be lost to the air.

Lids snapped wide, and her dark brown eyes
bloated. Callum held his breath, waiting to see
which way her reaction would fall. He prayed for
her joy but knew better.

"Don't say that." Jillian shoved his hand
away and scrambled to sit. "Don't you dare say that
to me."

Why did she have to be as stubborn as he
could be? Because he was. He'd held on to a secret
for so long. Even now, when he knew he'd have to
use it for any hope of having Jillian as his own, he
didn't want to. He wanted her to come to him on
her own, to release her loyalty to Amery, open her
eyes, and see her friend for the person she was, not
the one Jillian lifted her up to be.

Callum sat but left the distance between
them. He scrubbed a hand over his face and then
the memorial tattoo to Amery and his fallen
brothers. His gaze found Jillian's, and he leaped.

"Amery and I were together only once in
Coronado."

"No." Jillian's head shook. A smile curved her
lips conflicting with the tears that slipped down her

cheeks. "You two were more than her usual barroom hookup."

"It was a barroom hookup; my first. I never let people get close to me. She was only the second person I'd ever been with." Callum let that sink in because it had been the place he and Amery had met, the one place the three of them hadn't been stationed together. "She came to me two months later and told me she was pregnant."

"I don't need the details. What does it matter now, anyway?" She pushed off the bed, but he grabbed her hand.

"There was no way I was going to father a child I'd never know. So I wore a condom. She didn't like it, but I wouldn't budge. The condom didn't break."

"What are you saying?" She slapped tears away and firmed her jaw. "No. You two were perfect together. No."

"Think of all the shit you've seen, Jillian. Think of all you've survived. No one is perfect. You of all people should know that."

"But..." Jillian buried her face in her hands. Her knees hit the edge of the mattress, and she folded into herself.

"I'm not trying to hurt you. I needed you to know, and I should have told you a long time ago. She should have told you, but the longer it went, the more she liked the idea that Ashlyn was mine. The longer I stared into that baby's face, the more I did too."

Jillian straightened. Her hands fell to her sides as anger screwed up her face.

"Ashlyn looks like you." She backhanded the air. "Fuck, she acts just like you."

"I raised her, and Amery had a type." He shrugged and gave her a wink.

"Before you, yeah, she sure did. An M.O. of love 'em and leave 'em before they left her." Jillian's shoulders eased from her ears. Her jaw slacked and waggled while her eyes darted this way and that, working things out.

"When did she tell you?"

Callum chuckled. "She never had to tell me. I'm a SEAL and will be forever, no matter who I work for. I'm no one's dope."

"So you raised another man's child." Jillian gasped all the air from the room.

"I knew Amery's background. She was a good person raised in an awful environment. I knew my background, and I never wanted another kid to grow up knowing someone walked away from them."

"Why tell me?" Jillian wiped the tears from the tip of her nose and shored her emotions. "Now that Amery is gone, no one can know. If the real father ever found out, he could petition for custody."

The thought had kept him awake more nights than the sorrow of Amery's passing. Even now, it flipped his guts.

"My name is on the birth certificate. I'm Ashlyn's dad, and I trust you."

Jillian smacked both hands onto her hips. It thrust her breasts forward and blurred out everything but her muscled hourglass figure.

"What if I had gotten crazy jealous that you were raising another couple's child?"

"I'm sorry." He let his gaze lock on her breasts. "You said something, but I didn't catch it." She grabbed an errant pillow from the foot of the bed and launched it at him.

"I'm being serious." She snarled.

"Me too." He licked his lips.

Finally, a full giggle sang its way out of her mouth. It was everything. She and his girls were everything.

"You wouldn't get crazy jealous." He smiled and shook his head. "You love those girls as much as I do, as much as your own."

Her giggle stalled. "If I ever had one, yeah."

They stared at each other for a long time without a word. It was her move. He'd made all he had, though he could pull a few out of his ass in a pinch.

The phone next to him rang.

The clock read 0600. He'd expected a good-news call earlier. He pressed the button for the speaker. "Yep?"

"Rise and shine," Jared growled over the line.

"The news is that good, huh?" Callum asked.

"Titan turned up nothing in any of the relative's homes of the original thieves." Jared huffed. "Delta got nothing out of the kitchen staff last night, and we haven't been able to track the guy who got the best of you last night."

Jillian rolled her eyes. "So he got the best of you too?"

"Someone's feeling better. Wonder why?" Jared jabbed right back.

"Fine. Truce," Jillian offered. "What do you need from us?"

"Parker and his wife, Lexi, are working on a code to undo all the shit this hacker asshole did and to track him. Both teams are combing through known associate's panty drawers to try to find a lead." Jared grumbled to someone in the office and then returned to the phone. "Jillian, you know bombs, and Callum, you know people. Figure out where they took it. I need a Hail Mary pass at this point, so anything that can help."

"We're on it." Callum ended the call, stood, and grabbed his pants off the floor.

"We are?" Jillian tossed her hands into the air. "I haven't the first clue where to look. I mean I'm still shoveling through the crazy shit you just dumped on me."

"You needed to know." He grabbed her long lace number and held it up.

"I'll wear something else, thank you."

"Good. Get it on and bring your bomb babe bag along." Callum pulled on his shirt and fastened a few buttons, but opted out of the tuck to hide the pistol and holster at the small of his back.

"Where are we going?" She wrestled her curvy ass into a pair of jeans.

"We got lucky in the kitchen last night, and it wasn't a coincidence. All this in-house maneuvering points there, so that's where we'll go."

"Delta already questioned them." Jillian pulled on one boot and then the other, grabbing a T-shirt from a drawer and pulling it on as she headed for the door.

He met her there, grabbed her bag, and offered it with a smile. "I haven't."

"Cocky much?" She smirked, tossing the strap onto one shoulder.

"You tell me." He stole a quick kiss, closed the door behind them, and headed for the elevator.

"Definitely too cocky for our good." She stabbed the call button.

They waited in silence but not long before a car showed and they stepped inside. She kept a few feet between them, faced the door like she was waiting to parachute, and even ignored his reflection in the glossy metal doors.

"Do you hate me for keeping the secret?"

"No." A huff pooched her cheeks. "But I'm kind of pissed at Amery." She pulled her hair back into a low ponytail and stared at the ceiling. "She made me think everything was so perfect between you two."

"We had a great life together, but you were wrong."

"Me?" Jillian placed a delicate hand over her bosom. "Impossible."

"You said she was the linchpin, but you were that for us."

She watched him in the reflection of the elevator doors but didn't say a word. If she needed to know how much he'd bet on their future, he wouldn't hold back. Last night, she'd unleashed the little devil on his shoulder, and that fucker knew exactly what he wanted.

Callum laid it all on the line with an easy smile. "If you ever decide you want to have a baby, I'm your guy."

Jillian slung her backpack onto both shoulders. "You should be an asshole. You've got the look and the upbringing."

"Didn't take."

"Too bad for both of us." The door opened and she set out to the kitchen at an angry pace.

When they entered the restaurant, Callum took the lead, mimicking her warpath walk. Two hostesses whispered behind their hands. Servers skittered out of the way. He ignored them and headed straight for the kitchen. He smacked either door with a palm and shoved them so hard one smacked into the wall and the other a long metal table lined with square containers of salad fixings.

Every head in the place swung his way and stared, except for one. The stranger wore a uniform from a company that supplied the kitchen's linens.

He looked at Callum for a second but just as quickly dropped his gaze and turned into the long hallway.

Callum's lead on this fella was greater than yesterday's, but still, his stomach churned at the thought of Jillian in danger. The woman herself was danger. She played with it every day with explosives large enough to obliterate her. He took off after the guy.

"Stay with me," he called over his shoulder.

"You stay with me, slowpoke." Jillian zipped up next to him. It was cute, really, but his legs were almost twice as long as hers were.

He pushed twice as hard as he had yesterday, refusing to let this asshole get away. The man's heels jogged furiously over the path he and Jillian had run not long ago. Only, this time, he closed the distance, and the man chose the exterior door instead of the office door, which had been left propped open.

The guy disappeared through the bright doorway. His high-pitched Arabic shouts begged for backup. He'd better have brought a large contingent because what Callum wouldn't decimate with his fists and well-placed bullets, Jillian would.

"Eyes peeled," Callum hollered back at her and dove through the open doorway. He landed on the son of a bastard's back five feet from the exit, too close to the large cargo truck parked in the bay with its trailer door rolled high. They careened over the dock's ledge.

For a second, Callum's two hundred and sixty pounds weighed nothing as it plummeted to the concrete below. He held tight to the man's collar and braced for impact. Homey's face absorbed the brunt of the fall, leaving the guy unconscious, if not dead. The truck's passenger door swinging wide kept him from a conclusive determination.

Black boots stomped onto the rusty metal grating above an auxiliary gas tank. Callum rolled off the probably dead guy—judging by the amount of blood and hint of brain matter seeping onto the ground—and ghosted under the rig. Everything inside him went quiet, even his panic over the absence of Jillian's voice or gunfire. It quieted to keep her safe, to eliminate the threats, and lay eyes on her right the fuck now.

Dark navy pants and boots matching the dead guy's ensemble hit the concrete in an athletic stance that meant business. It lasted one step before faltering. "Arif? Arif, get up," the passenger ordered.

Callum pushed and coiled onto the balls of his feet and waited for the man to pass his hideout. The narrow barrel and blunted shark fin sight of an AK-47 lowered by the man's side. Jillian had to be inside the building. There was no way she wouldn't have fired unless she were also hiding or caught. He hadn't heard her scream. He needed this fucker to get a move on. His muscles itched for release for the unknown.

The passenger stopped even with Callum. He didn't want to use his gun because it would draw more attention. Still, he reached for the handle. The man dropped to a knee, pressing his AK's barrel against the ground. His hand extended toward the body. Callum abandoned his gun and launched himself at the terrorist.

He coiled his legs around the man's torso, pinning his falling body to the ground. One palm wrapped around the guy's jaw and the other braced a black thatch of hair. He wrenched.

It was over in an instant.

Callum searched the dock. No Jillian. He scrambled back to peer inside the rig's cab. Nothing. His heart rate ratcheted with each passing second he didn't find her pouty mouth and long dark hair. Sweat coated his palms as though it were his first mission, first kill—well, first two. Though he hadn't meant to kill the runner. They needed someone to question to find the warhead, but before he found that hunk of metal, he had to find Jillian.

Determination churned his legs to the dock. Conditioning hoisted him over it and toward the doorway where he'd launched himself through three minutes ago. Where the hell was—

"I give my life to Allah." The thickly accented declaration echoed from behind.

Callum turned toward the truck. The same man from last night stood at the mouth of the trailer's open cargo space. Sweat dripped from his chin. His hands shook, making his fingers fumble with the last clasp on a suicide vest.

Christ, his wobbly hands alone could detonate the homemade device. Forget about the remote curled into his palm.

"I give it to stop the infidels." Two halves of the clasp slid together. The man raised his hand high, glared at Callum, and drew his last breath.

Chapter Eleven

Jillian kept pace with Callum, considering his stride easily bested hers by a foot and a half. They blew past the prep tables, ovens, stunned staff, a raving chef, and the commercial grade refrigerator. The bright metal door flashed like a neon sign that read, 'Hello, dumb asses?'

Her feet compounded their own weight and dragged her to a standstill. Callum pushed on around the corner after the fleeing man, taking her heart with him. She stood with her hand on the lever and struggled with the measure of her options. One, go with the man she loved and make sure he was safe. Two, open the door and find the warhead capable of killing thousands—both of them included.

She gnashed her teeth, looked right to find the staff down the hallway already back in their gourmet breakfast prep mode, and jerked the door wide. Condensing vapors rose from the ground as they had in Titan's subterranean cooler. Why hadn't she thought to look here? It was so simple yet so obvious, it wasn't. She stepped into the curling clouds. Then again, if the entire staff wasn't in on it, why hadn't one of them alerted management about the large bomb sitting next to their orange-spotted trevally?

If the entire kitchen staff was on the terrorist's payroll, what was there to keep them from locking her in here, and letting her slowly freeze to death? Jillian hesitated in the doorway, wishing like hell that she could see the whole of the freezer's contents from her vantage point.

Deep shelves with crates of fresh fruits, vegetables, and meats lined the walls on either side of the entrance, limiting her view. She leaned out of the cooler and looked left, yearning for Callum's face to appear from around the corner. No way could she wait for him even if she wanted. When he didn't magically appear, she pulled both pearls from her earlobes, set them deliberately at the base of the wall outside the refrigerator, and prayed he came back soon and noticed them.

Then she dipped into the cold.

The dim light above the door did little to illuminate the refrigerator's contents...and still, disappointment socked her in the gut. None of the shelves or crates held a deadly surprise unless Titan was planning to take down trans fats and sugar.

"Goddammit." Jillian double punched the air and paced the perimeter of the slick concrete floor. Why else would there be such a link to the kitchen, unless the thieves utilized the massive hotel cooler?

It didn't make sense. None of this added up. Frustration crawled over her skin like a thousand baby tarantulas. She snagged a lime from a bin and launched it at the far wall.

A hollow gong reverberated in the contained space. It gave rise to a sleep deprived, post goose egg headache that rivaled all others. The unusual sound also piqued her interest.

Jillian slung her backpack to her front and yanked a flashlight from it. When she clicked it on, the small light cast a high beam. She ran it along the seam where the metal wall met the metal ceiling. Irritation pounded behind her eyes. She dropped the beam to the floor.

"Got you, fuckers." Her headache eased immediately at the sight of shallow scrapes behind the row of shelves where the wall had been moved forward to make room for something behind it.

She pocketed the flashlight, hurried to the corner shelving unit, which non-coincidentally held a light load of finished desserts. Her fingers wrapped around the cold metal and heaved it from the wall. At the bottom corner, a notch had been cut into the sheet of chrome.

"I win." Jillian pulled back the false wall panel and stared into the darkness. Her pulse thumped in her neck. She snatched the flashlight from her pocket and swept from right to left.

A wooden frame held the fake wall in place, leaving a three-foot gap between the insulation and the metal plates that ran the length of the six-foot room. It made the perfect nook for the warhead she'd rescued from the clutches of evil once before.

"Hello, beautiful." She swallowed past the joy and panic of having the ultimate lethal weapon at her fingertips, slipped into the nook, and wedged herself between the insulation and freezing metal— wedged atop a serving cart—that was meant to arm a submarine.

There was no way to know if someone had a remote detonator on the thing. She'd love to call for backup for herself and Callum. In the cold, dark space with no pistol, she was a sitting duck for whoever came through the door, and there was no way to know what kind of situation Callum was running into. Her gaze lifted to the door as her mind momentarily locked on the man she loved beyond understanding. She couldn't, wouldn't risk leaving its side until she'd dismantled the mechanisms for kaboom.

Jillian slipped off her pack and laid it gently atop the warhead. The zipper was as cold as a windshield wiper on a winter day. It screamed across the track as she opened the bag wide and let her fingers dance across the tightly organized tools. Her eyes surveilled the lower belly for the Hallelujah panel—as in, hallelujah I probably won't die today.

"Number six spanner head. Cocksuckers." Jillian hissed and snagged the one and only such screwdriver from her bag.

The damn things were notorious for breaking, especially when using on overtightened screws or the metal was cold. She ground her teeth and ignored the sting of frozen metal against the pads of her fingers.

A concussive blast roared through the building. Outside the nook, plates and cookware rattled, crates toppled, and people screamed. Jillian braced a hand on her bag and another over her heart.

"Callum." His name squeaked out as an oath.

Her fingers shook, and her heart rattled against her ribs, demanding release.

Jillian straightened and placed the screwdriver in the notch of the first screw. A sob gathered strength in her chest. Tears slipped down her cheeks onto her bare wrists. She suppressed the quivering of her lungs, her sniffles, her impending sorrow, and gingerly twisted. The screw held fast, like she did to the hope that the bomb wasn't as large as the boom she'd heard, and that Callum had been far, far away from it.

"Fuck you. Fuck it all." Jillian screamed and sobbed and shook her fists into the air.

Footfalls thundered through the cooler. She grabbed the heaviest wrench from her bag and prayed it was enough.

"Not everyone, baby." Callum huffed in the false wall's doorway. "Just me."

Jillian launched the wrench to the right of Callum's blood splattered form. "Don't ever scare me like that again."

"Hey." Callum tossed up both hands. "I looked back, and you weren't there. So back at ya, babe."

"The explosion?" Her body couldn't keep up with her attitude. Every muscle quivered with relief.

"They were coming to transport the warhead or blow us all to hell trying. The last man standing had a suicide vest."

"And..." She gulped.

"I shot him and the lever, holding open the trailer door, which locked him inside, and I ran like hell." He nodded at the warhead. "Now, disarm this thing so we can go home to our girls."

Her heart fainted at the elation and horror of having everything she'd ever wanted. She stood in a stupor, unable to operate the simplest of tools to save everyone in a five-mile radius.

"Come on, Jillian. You can do it." He might have meant go back home with him and live with his girls, but his warm hands guided hers to the first screw.

For the first time in her life, Jillian drew from his steady strength. One by one, she unfastened the screws and eased back the metal square.

"Holy shit," Callum whispered.

"Maybe I can't run as fast as you, but I can RSP a bomb better than you can." Jillian kept her eyes on the mechanical fuse and electronic accelerometer.

"I have no idea what that means, but it's hot as fuck."

A smile tugged at Jillian's lips. She let it stay, while she praised all the gods that no one had installed booby traps, and cracked the appropriate circuit boards in the panel.

"We need to get Titan in here to secure this thing." She slipped her screwdriver back into her pack and looked at Callum.

"In a minute." He threw his arms around her and squeezed the breath from her lungs. His face nuzzled against her neck.

"I love you, Jillian."

Chapter Twelve

If he were the bare-knuckle badass he showed the world, then having Jillian ignore his second profession of love wouldn't hurt so much. Too fucking bad. Pain, he could handle. No matter how long it took her to overcome Amery's ghost and see them as a couple, he'd wait. He wouldn't wait because he was conceited or desperate, but rather because he knew she loved him and his girls with everything she possessed. It was in the way she made love to him, the way she looked at him, the way she danced from foot to foot, waiting for the rest of Delta and Titan to trickle out of the hotel kitchen.

Most of the guys had gone to the basement to secure the warhead, but a few had stayed behind to irritate the shit out of him. Well, that was just one. The damn Aussie was trying to die today. If he eyeball fucked Jillian one more time, he was about to oblige.

"Parker, scan every face before they come back inside this hotel. I want zero unknowns in here; guest and staff alike." Jared stood in the chaos of strewn food with both hands on his hips, slinging orders as if it was a battlefield. "Delta, you're on crowd control."

"What about them?" Ryder pointed at him and Jillian.

"Bradfield's officially no longer my business, and Jillian can do whatever the hell she wants with the rest of her day." Jared shrugged. "Thanks to her, we have this one. Now, get after it."

Ryder fell out with the rest of the crew through the double doors.

"The jet is fueled and ready whenever you are." Jared split a look between him and Jillian. "Or you can stay. I can always use another capable and trusted hand around here."

Jilly dance shuffled some more.

"One condition, though." Jared offered his hand.

"What's that?" Callum shook the sturdy arm and quirked a brow.

Jared's gaze slid to Jillian and her uncomfortable shimmy shake. "Tell Vail Tucker why you're really coming halfway across the world. I don't want to deal with him if he thinks I poached one of his guys."

"Yes, sir." Callum tried to hide his smile, but it only half worked.

"Cooper, amazing work today." Jared extended his hand to Jillian.

"Thank you, sir," she squeaked.

"On the same token, if you want to renegotiate your contract or home base, let me know." Jared dipped his head and shoved through the doors before Jillian's jaw hit the floor.

Callum grabbed her hand and pulled it to his chest. He waited for several beats for the silence to settle around them. After the chaos of the morning, it was a welcomed quiet for talk of the future.

"We can work," he whispered.

Jillian finally stilled her feet and looked at him. Her chest rose and fell with a long breath and then another.

"I love you, Callum. I just can't go back there and live a life meant for my friend." Before his mouth could open, she lifted a palm and pushed on. "I've never been able to make a simple relationship work, much less this." She pressed the hand already on his chest harder against him, and then pulled it away, placing it over her heart.

"The baggage of our pasts won't allow this to work." Her wisp-riddled ponytail swung back and forth.

Irritation seeped into his words. "I made it work with Amery, when we barely knew one another, when she was pregnant, an obligation, and not much more at the start."

"I know." She sobbed. "I know, but what if we can't make it work? I'd never be able to leave the girls. Then we'd all be miserable." Jillian's lashes clumped together with tears. She slapped the moisture from her cheeks and smiled up at him. "If we could stay here forever and live in our little world, where you're mine, and I'm yours, maybe. But going back...It's just too much."

"I've never seen you run away from anything, not even Trent the asshole." Full-blown anger burned his gut. He wanted nothing more than to pull her into his arms and soothe her fears, but she was shoving him away.

"Don't you get it? You're more important than anything before."

"Then don't run away." Callum couldn't keep the pleading from his voice and didn't much care.

"I'm not."

But she was.

Jillian stood on her tippy toes and pressed her lips to his for one heartbreaking second. "I'm staying. You're going."

"Goddammit, Jillian." He grabbed her shoulders and pulled her close. "You are mine, and I am yours, from this day until my last." He shook her, not hard, but fuck, he wanted her to understand. "Don't you get it? You're it for me."

"And you for me." Tears continued to cascade down her face, telling him everything he needed to know. She wasn't leaving with him.

Callum planted a hand at her nape. He pressed his mouth to hers and dared her not to participate. They kissed like starved animals, gnashing and sucking at each other for life. When her hands pressed to his heart, he pushed back.

Jillian heaved breaths. Her wild eyes begged, but for what, he couldn't be sure. Callum took one long last look, turned, and walked out.

Chapter Thirteen

Two months and two days later...

Jillian's lower quads and back screamed as she leaned over the network of wires partially buried in the dirt that linked three packs of ammunition. Next to her, Boomer bit back a pitchy whine.

"It's okay, Boom Boom. You're the only one making any racket today." She soothed the only family she had since she'd pushed Callum away. The stocky pit bull held his position—sitting just outside the blast radius—but quirked his head. "Give me one minute and we'll be clear."

It was quite astounding that he could hear her through her full-face helmet and specialized bodysuit. Growing up, Jillian hadn't had a steady house, much less a pet rock. She didn't get the dog, but she loved him already. Boomer could read her mood in an instant and dealt with her accordingly. If she was excited, he bounced so high he threatened to touch the ceiling of her suite. If she was sad, he curled his massive body as close to her as he could manage, which usually meant on top of her, and settled in for the long haul. The poor thing hadn't seen her happy, no more than he could make her. He did as well as he could.

Jared hadn't said the bomb-detecting love-muffin was a pity gift, but she had her suspicions.

The first of which being the timing of Boomer's appearance. If she'd known two weeks of moping would have gotten her a comrade in the never-ending fight against VO-IEDs, she'd have done it sooner. Moped, not pushed away the man she loved.

She reached the network with wire cutters and moved forward with the render safe procedure. It only took forty seconds.

"Clear," she said into the helmet's communications system.

Boomer yipped his approval.

"That's got to be a world record," Danny awed.

"I know, right?" Jack agreed.

The fresh-faced, fresh out of school EODs Jared had given her to help out—a.k.a. train—awed and guffawed through the channel.

"Bringing it your way." Jillian collected each pack of ammunition one at a time and deposited it into the bomb box for them to destroy.

"I've lost count of how many boxes you've filled in the last three days." Jack closed the lid, shook his head, and sighed.

"We're losing sun. Let's get these last ones destroyed and get back to HQ." Jillian removed her helmet and turned to Boomer. Despite her aching muscles, she fell to her knees and opened her arms. "Come, boy."

Boomer raced across the distance and eased enough before impact that he didn't knock her completely over. He sniffed her hair and rubbed himself against the front of her suit.

"You're a good boy. The best, Boom Boom." She rubbed his neck and patted his belly. "Are you hungry?" His ears perked. "Want to go home?" It wasn't exactly her home, but it was as close as she'd get to one. Boomer bounced off her. "Load up." He nearly spun out in his haste to get to her Jeep.

"Hey, Coop?" Danny called. When she turned around, his hand was extended and in it a comms link. "Boss Man."

They weren't officially Titan, though they lived in Titan's Eastern HQ, used Titan toys, and were paid by Titan money. They weren't the team, but they'd play with the team anytime the need arose. Until then, they cleared the streets and communities of deadly explosives.

Jillian pressed the wireless piece into her ear and started peeling off her suit. "Cooper here."

"Let the boys demo and head in," Jared ordered. "I have a surprise for you."

"Absolutely not. The last two times you've had surprises my entourage has grown. I didn't take this job to train an army of EODs for you."

"Why did you take the job, Jillian?"

Jared didn't often use her first name, but when he did, it was always a well-placed blow.

"To simplify my life, and here you are trying to make it more complicated," she snapped.

"Life, by definition, isn't simple. Are you going to live it or have a bomb take you to the next place to be with your friend, whose shadow you exist under?"

"I'm fine. I'm not—"

"Right. You're fine, which is why you spent the last three days—the days on either side of and the day of your best friend's one-year anniversary— digging up IEDs from dawn till dust, carelessly surpassing reg limits with your K-9 and comrades," Jared snarled over the line. "Get back here and figure out your answer to the question on the way."

Jillian tossed the comms link back to Danny.

Surprisingly, he caught the link and tipped his imaginary hat to her with it. "We'll take care of things here."

"Thanks," she growled as she tore off the rest of her ABS and climbed into the driver's seat.

Boomer danced in the passenger seat, amazing her yet again that his big ass could move around so much and not fall out the window.

"Hey, Boom." She retrieved his water bottle and turned it up for him. The fella guzzled like a beer pong champion. "Good, huh?" His long pink tongue lolled out and slathered the excess water off his jaws in affirmation.

The car rumbled to life, and she turned to look at her dog. She'd signed papers for him and everything, saying that he'd retire to her and move and live with her unless she died. "Callum's your protector if I die." Jillian pressed her face into Boomer's neck. "I don't want to die. I want to live." He licked a wide path over her shoulder. His little thanks for not giving up.

Why had she given up on her and Callum without a fight? He was right not to let her talk to the girls and not beg her—more than he had in that kitchen—to give them a chance. She was the one who could have said what she wanted, and he'd have happily given it to her.

"In the back, Boom." She shifted into gear and stared at the wide, sweet face staring back at her. "Now. Rules are rules."

He scooted into the backseat and hunkered down, out of sight. To the right or, in this case, very wrong people, the bounty of Boomer's head was greater than the one on hers.

The Jeep shimmied and bumped over the straight line back to the road. She hooked a right and drove. The wind blew through her ponytail, drying the sweat from her skin and slicked back hair. Boomer bit it as it streamed from the front seat for a couple of minutes before he sacked out.

They kicked up dust as far as the rearview could see until they hit the first village. Jillian slowed to accommodate the people on foot walking to and from the market at the center of town. As she neared the outskirts, a little boy caught her eye.

He was no more than six. A smile stretched his mouth, and his feet beat against the dirt with impressive speed as he chased after a paper ball the size of his head. The ball rolled and rolled to the far side of the rubble lot. When the boy caught up to it, he turned, levered back his foot, and kicked it back the other way.

Weeks ago, the town had been a scampering whisper of what it was today. Weeks ago, she, Boomer, Danny, and Jack had come through, clearing eight bomb boxes worth of IEDs as they went from a war long forgotten by the world but not the people of the UAE and Oman border town.

This place needed her more than the States ever had, but she needed Callum and the girls more than she'd needed anything in her entire life. Amery and fear be damned.

She'd made the right decision to stay but had been too afraid of his rejection, of the stress she'd put on the girls, to ask him to stay and raise his family away from everything they knew.

Boomer snored in the backseat, while Jillian formed the finer details of a plan for the two-hour ride back to Titan HQ. By the time she'd pulled into the secure parking at the rear entrance, she knew exactly what she had to do and finally had the courage to do it. All it had taken was time away, a love that refused to fade, and a well-placed question.

The moment she killed the engine, Boomer yawned and stretched his way to standing. "You ready for the negotiation of a lifetime, Boom?" He yipped. "Me too. Let's go."

Jillian secured her gear and bags in the basement locker room, grimaced at her reflection—sweat-slicked hair and dirt rimmed everything. She paused long enough to splash water on her face and wipe the desert off before she continued on to the elevator and hit the button for the war room. Her loyal companion parked his butt at her heel. He stared up with panted breaths and a hanging tongue.

"We can do this." The fur of the tip of his ear soothed the pads of her fingers and her jittery nerves. She had no reason to be jittery. Either Jared would agree, or she'd quit and move back to the States.

Gosh, she didn't want to move back. She just wanted her family here, with her.

The doors opened onto the floor that housed Titan's war room, Parker's tech lair away from his tech lair, and some other rooms she'd hadn't been inside. She braced herself, nodded at Boomer, and pressed forward. The closer she walked to the door of choice, the smaller the hall became.

"What the hell?" Jillian shook out her fingers, which trembled at her side. Boomer pressed his head into her palm and gave her the strength to choose the future she wanted. "You're the best, Boom. Here we go."

She pushed through the door with a full breath ready to tell Jared what was what but stalled in the doorway. Her jaw hit the floor. Every ounce of I'm-going-to-tell-Jared-what's-what cascaded onto the short carpet with it.

"Jillian." A woman with perfect breasts strapped so high into a tank top they nearly grazed her chin propped a hip on the conference table. Not weird at all, considering the men Titan employed were rumored to have smokin' hot women in their lives. But this one cradled a baby against her shoulder and a pistol on her hip. The two ends of the spectrum didn't compute.

Her bright red lips stretched into a devious smile. "What, am I supposed to be at home barefoot and pregnant with the next one?"

Jillian screwed her jaw back into place. "No, I —"

"Oh, come on. I'm not going to bite unless you try to kidnap my baby." She smoothed a hand down one thigh of her leather pants. "Even then I wouldn't bite. I'd shoot."

"Sugar?"

"Of course." She nodded at her baby. "I think it's safe to say, I'm not the Virgin Mary."

A soft, rich chuckle rumbled through Sugar's lips. Her gaze dropped to her baby's face. The tone of her laughter immediately shifted to an easy cooing sigh. She leaned in close to the bundle's face and inhaled deeply. The jokes and sarcasm melted away, revealing a hint of the adoring mother she was when she wasn't busting balls.

Boomer looked up at Jillian and shifted on his feet, as though to say, 'It isn't polite to stand in doorways.' She walked to the nearest corner of the table and stopped with her life support at her heel. Not since Callum left had she ever been so confused. Agitation shot a wave of gooseflesh across her arms. She had things to do, and already they weren't going to plan.

"The pretty doggy!" A sweet, high-pitched voice that didn't belong to her girls knocked her between the eyes with desperate need, the need to be with Aria and Ashlyn.

Jared waltzed—as much as she'd ever seen him—into the room hand in hand with his stepdaughter, Asal.

"Can I go pet the pretty doggy, Daddy?" Asal offered up the widest smile meant for melting hearts.

"You almost got me with those big brown eyes." He chucked her chin and blew her a kiss. "But we have to wait, just a minute."

Boss Man—and Asal by default, though her eyes were locked on Boomer—stopped at his wife's side, caressed her hair and slipped his gaze to his baby. The total badassness of Jared Westin didn't fall away; if anything, it grew with ferocity next to his woman and children—children that weren't all biologically his. As though he loved so much it bolstered him as a leader and man.

Their family offered Jillian a glimpse—in perfect clarity—of the insignificance of maternity and paternity. A family wasn't always made up of DNA. Those details were inconsequential. Her foster fuck-ups along the way hadn't shown her that, but Amery and Callum had.

She never wanted to claim her family as much as she did at that moment, and a surprise she didn't understand stood between her and that petition. "Your family is lovely, but I don't understand the relevance of the surprise?"

Reluctantly, or maybe mischievously, Jared's gaze left his wife's naughty grin and assessed her. "Have you thought about what I—"

"Yes, I really need to talk to you about a few things." Jillian usually didn't talk over her superiors, but now that she'd made a decision, she couldn't wait around. The need to move crawled all over her. "First, I need some leave, maybe two weeks, and then I need to find a house here or in a nearby village, a safe one. The hotel is nice, but it's not the place for a dog, much less—"

"Jillian." Jared held up his hand. His tone and the gesture combined rocketed her heart into her throat, which was fine. He didn't want her to speak anyway.

Boomer chose that moment to break his hold and abandon her side. Everything was going to shit.

"She's my surprise, not yours," Jared said.

"Yep, I hitched a ride." Sugar hooked a finger in Jared's blue jeans and pulled him back to her side.

"I..." Jillian's head shook. She didn't understand, but she'd already said that. Maybe she should just grab a chair and watch as her plans were cut into ribbons, and then hold them high over her head and announce her resignation.

Boomer whined, drawing her gaze to the door Jared and Asal had walked through. He pawed at the threshold and whined again. Even though it wasn't his alert for explosives, Jillian's heartbeat thundered in her esophagus. Just like he fed off her energy, she fed off his, read and reacted. It kept them alive.

She swallowed her heart and glared at Jared. "What's going on?"

"It looks like he found your surprise, which is also his." A satisfied smile stretched his mouth.

Chapter Fourteen

Callum kicked back and watched the drama unfold on a screen in front of him. Sure, spying on Jillian while Sugar and Jared toyed with her emotions was devious and not at all the frontal attacks he'd always dealt her. He was a SEAL. SEALs got shit done covertly. With his little girls' hearts and happiness on the line, he dealt the woman he loved a little subterfuge to even the playing field.

He leaned forward and bumped the volume in his earbuds. Aria and Ashlyn sat on the floor beside him and placed multicolored beads on a thin cord, pandering to their newfound jewelry obsession. No way would he miss Jillian's answer to the question. If only Jared would stop making googly eyes at his wife and baby long enough to pose it.

Finally, the guy eased off them and looked at Jillian. "Have you thought about what I—"

"Yes," she cut him off.

Oh, shit. This was either a really good sign or really fucking horrible one. Callum's asshole puckered so much he nearly sucked up the chair.

Jillian charged on without a breath, but the world seemed to leave her lips in slow motion. "I really need to talk to you about a few things." She lifted a finger. "First, I need some leave, maybe two weeks, and then I need to find a house here or in a nearby village, a safe one. The hotel is nice, but it's not the place for a dog, much less—"

Why the fuck did Jared stop her? Callum's nose was inches from the screen begging the words to fall off Jillian's lips as though he were a deranged soap opera fanatic. He couldn't give two fucks right now that Sugar hitched a ride across the ocean with them. She was a great woman and all, but he needed Jillian to finish that thought, now.

His palms braced either side of the monitor.

"Dude, hands off," Parker chided him as though he were a toddler with sticky fingers.

"I'm not going to crush it." Callum released the computer. He didn't offer the guy an apology, but he did give him a very manly eye roll.

His girls were rubbing off on him.

"I'm not so sure." Parker pointed at the door.

The girls had abandoned their craft post and breached the front line without orders or even permission. His stomach hit the button for the ground floor, and his palms slicked with sweat.

Christ, he'd stormed battlefields and infiltrated enemy camps with no more than a handful of men. Jillian shouldn't scare him this much. He stood and hurried to the door but stopped.

"Boomy!" Ashlyn launched herself at the dog they'd visited almost weekly since he was born but hadn't seen in two months.

"I've missed you so much." Aria wrapped her arms around the dog and her sister and squeezed tight enough to render anyone else unconscious.

Laughs and giggles spirited the air and Callum held his breath. Jared's eyes shifted from the girls to Jillian at the other end of the room and back too many times.

"Girls." Jillian's emotion-soaked voice didn't question their appearance. It reveled in their presence.

"Jilly! Oh, my gosh, Jilly!" Aria abandoned her sister and Boomer as quickly as she'd attacked them and sprinted out of sight. "I've missed you more."

"Jilly?" Ashlyn looked from Boomer to Jillian and covered her tiny mouth. Tears flowed over her cheeks, and a joyful sob rocked her.

It broke his heart into a thousand pieces.

"Ashlyn, baby. Oh, please don't cry." Jillian stormed into view with Aria wrapped protectively in her arms. She collapsed to her knees and collected Ashlyn to her chest. "My girls. Oh, my God, my girls."

Jillian had ordered the ban on tears, but they seeped from her tired eyes.

"I'm so happy," Ashlyn wailed, sounding the exact opposite.

"Me too." Jillian held the girls to her chest, pressed their heads onto either shoulder, and rocked them as she'd done since they were infants.

Just like that, his heart welded together stronger than it had ever been. No matter what came out of Jillian's mouth, she loved him and his girls. Everything else would fall into place.

Sugar sniffled, but when he looked up, she blinked furiously and hugged her girls tight, while Jared did the same to all three.

Minutes passed with the girls hugging and rocking until Aria wiped her tears away and sat back in Jillian's arms. "Don't go away from us again. A little trip is all right, I guess, but never move away. Always be where we are, no matter where in the world we are."

He loved her to-the-point approach.

Jillian's pink lips parted and then closed. Her gaze lifted and speared his heart, not to maim but capture, he prayed. "Wherever we are in the world?"

Callum stepped into the room and nodded, unwilling to speak his mind until the girls were out of earshot.

She settled her gaze on Aria. "I promise. Where you go, I go."

"Forever?" Aria pushed.

"Until you're grown and you don't want me to." Jillian smiled and pressed kisses to each of the girls' foreheads.

"I'll never not want you with me," Aria assured her.

"Me either," Ashlyn agreed.

"That sounds perfect." Jillian laughed. The warmth of it set his soul aflame. She braced the girls' faces in her hands and caressed their cheeks. They melted into her.

"Okay." Sugar blotted at her mascara, stood, and grinned at the girls. "Who wants ice cream?"

The room erupted with giggles and cheers. Boomer bounded on his haunches as though it were a high jump contest. He won, hands down. Jared even gave a, "Heck, yeah." The girls raced for the door with Asal—with whom they'd made fast friends on the flight over—but stopped in the doorway with Sugar and looked back.

Jillian stood. "I'm going to talk with your daddy for a few minutes, and then we'll be there. Promise. Save me some, okay?"

"I'll try," Aria snickered.

"Jilly, can Boomer come with me for the ice cream?" Ashlyn gripped his collar so firmly, her pudgy little fingers turned red and white.

"Absolutely, but he can't have any. No matter how much he asks, okay?" Jillian lifted her gaze to Jared for a ten-four.

"Wait for me." Parker pulled the tech lab door closed behind him and rushed past them to bring up the rear. "I could go for some vanilla. Might even splurge with chocolate sauce." He closed the war room door on their dispute of the best ice cream flavors, isolating him and Jillian in the space.

"Somehow, I get the impression my dog is really Ashlyn's dog?" Jillian stood next to the conference table with both hands pressed into fists at her side. Neither her shoulders, nor her wide eyes, nor her slight smile said angry.

Reserved, maybe.

"Jared gave him to you because I didn't think you'd take him if you'd known he came from me."

Her fist flattened out and shot to her rounded mouth. "But, Callum, those dogs aren't cheap."

"Relax. We, the girls and I, rescued him from the shelter when he was still a puppy, a huge puppy. A guy I worked with owed me a favor, and his father happened to be a top-notch trainer."

Tears welled in her eyes and her hand stayed fastened over her mouth. "How long?"

"Two months after the funeral." Callum stuffed his hands in his pockets to keep from launching himself at her as Aria had.

"Why didn't you tell me?" Her lips peeked out from her fingertips.

"It was a surprise. The girls and I visited him all the time. I just knew one of them was going to blab, but they wanted to make you smile as much as I did." He took a step closer, unable to stop himself. "I was going to warm you up to the idea of a dog after the cemetery, but...things didn't work out like I'd planned."

"Yeah, plans." Jillian gave a trilling, derisive sigh. "They always go to shit, don't they?" She posed her question to his shoes but then slowly lifted her gaze. Her fingers fell away, revealing a smile that bloomed as wide and bright as he'd ever seen it. "And sometimes, those plans fall apart to make room for something else; something different and unexpected but no less beautiful or worthwhile."

She took a step closer to him. "I was coming here to ask Jared for time off so I could go to the States, claim my family, and—"

Oh, hell no. No more waiting. Those words hit him in the center bull's-eye. Callum snatched her to his chest, locked his arms around her, and sealed his mouth to hers. Jillian devoured him as if she hadn't eaten in days. Her fingers bit into his neck and back. Tears tickled his cheeks.

"I am yours, Jillian," he growled against her mouth.

"Wait," she panted.

"I've been waiting so damn long."

She braced his face in her palms and pled with her eyes. He moaned against her cheek but stilled with a hand wrapped around her ponytail. "Yes, ma'am?"

"I know how much I'm about to ask of you, but..."

"Ask, Jillian. If it's in my power to give it to you, it's yours," he promised.

"Like Aria said, no matter where we are in the world, I want you and the girls to be with me. I want to be with you. I want us to be a family...here, for now. Maybe some place else later, but I want us to start fresh together."

"I didn't hear a question." Callum released her hair and pressed a finger to Jillian's full lips

that parted on a rejoinder. "I didn't need to. In case
our appearance on the other side of the globe
wasn't gesture enough, maybe this will be."

He set her on her feet, bent a knee for the
first time, and stole Jillian's hand as it made its
way to her mouth.

"The girls and I decided we wanted you,
wherever and however we could get you. We sold
the house, bought dog toys, a hell of a lot of luggage
—most of it pink—and one more thing before we
left."

"Callum." Jillian sighed.

He fished out the ring he'd scoured jewelry
stores and artists' galleries for a month to find. The
copper-finished medium width band reminded him
of all the wires she'd cut or lost in her lifetime. This
one, their relationship, wouldn't be severed. It
formed a protective metal box around the stone at
the center, around Jillian, and still allowed her
brilliance to shine through.

"Jillian, we've never had anything
conventional in our lives. But we have trust and
understanding, laughter and love, two stunning
girls and a dog together. I choose you here or
anywhere in the world, as long as we're together. Be
our future?"

Her hand quaked in his. Breaths rushed in
and out of her chest. Moisture dripped off the tip of
her nose.

"You are mine. I am yours today until my
dying day." She nodded furiously. "Yes."

Callum pressed the ring onto her finger and
eased her onto his knee. His palm cupped the back
of her neck. Her lips warmed his. She tasted like
charcoal, sulfur, dirt, and home. He eased his
tongue between her lips for a deeper taste. He
pulled her close until the outside of her thigh

brushed his burgeoning hard-on. She leaned into him, pressing her chest to his and sucking his tongue.

"I've missed you, Jillian. I need you."

Jillian pulled back, gasping. "I suppose we need to go have ice cream?"

"Fuck the ice cream." Callum stood and shifted two chairs out of the way with his boot. He laid her on the conference room table and spread her legs wide.

"Here? Now?" She gestured to the room and her dusty clothes.

Like some desert dirt would stop him from getting close to his woman. He settled his erection at the juncture of her hips and leaned over until his face was a breath away from hers.

"Always. Anywhere," he growled and set about claiming his very-soon-to-be bride.

ENEMY MINE
A BASE BRANCH NOVEL

When friends become enemies and enemies become lovers.

Born in the blood of Sierra Leone's Civil War, enslaved, then sold to the US as an orphan, Base Branch operative Sloan Harris is emotionally dead and driven by vengeance. With no soul to give, her body becomes the bargaining chip to infiltrate a warlord's inner circle. The man called The Devil killed her family and helped destroy a region.

As son of the warlord, Baine Kendrick will happily use Sloan's body if it expedites his father's demise. Yet, he is wholly unprepared for the possessive and protective emotions she provokes. Maybe it's the flashes of memory … two forgotten children drawing in the dirt beneath the boabab tree… But he fears there is more at stake than his life.

In the Devil's den with Baine by her side, Sloan braves certain death and discovers a spirit for living.

FOR ALL TO SEE
A BUREAU NOVEL

Pristine waters and purified evil.

Two by two, dark-haired beauties vanish only to reappear as hanging, plundered corpses. The Virgin Islands boast diamond-white beaches, lush green mountains, a rich cultural heritage—and a brutal killer.

Three years on the "Field-Dresser" case and Special Agent Nathan Brewer is days away from catching the bastard—if he can convince a certain brunette to trust him. Only the woman is more likely to take a casual stroll on the surface of the sun.

After fleeing her troubles in the United States for the quiet life of a school teacher on the island of Tortola, Madelyn Garrett never imagined she'd be fixated upon by pure evil.

In a fight for her life—with a dwindling number of friends—she must rely on her cunning and Nathan's skills for survival.

Megan Mitcham was born and raised among the live oaks and shrimp boats of the Mississippi Gulf Coast, where her enormous family still calls home. She attended college at the University of Southern Mississippi where she received a bachelor's degree in curriculum, instruction, and special education. For several years Megan worked as a teacher in Mississippi. She married and moved to South Carolina and began working for an international non-profit organization as an instructor and co-director.

In 2009 Megan fell in love with books. Until then, books had been a source for research or the topic of tests. But one day she read *Mercy* by Julie Garwood. And oh, Mercy, she was hooked!

Megan lives in Southern Arkansas where she pens heart pounding romantic thriller novels and window-steaming erotic romance. For information on releases and giveaways subscribe at meganmitcham.com!

Facebook: AuthorMeganMitcham
Twitter: @MeganMMMitcham
Pinterest: MeganMitcham5
Goodreads: Megan_Mitcham
Website: www.meganmitcham.com

FOR INFORMATION ON NEW RELEASES & GIVEAWAYS, SIGN UP FOR MEGAN'S NEWSLETTER AT WWW.MEGANMITCHAM.COM.